pipedreams

By

Joanna C. Smith

This is a work of fiction. Names, characters, places and incidents either are the product of the author's imagination or are used fictitiously, and any resemblance to actual persons, living or dead, events or locales is entirely coincidental.

Second printing 2006.

Copyright © 2004 by Joanna C. Smith.
Printed in the United States. All rights reserved.

ISBN 1-58597-254-1

Library of Congress Control Number: 2004102407

4500 College Boulevard
Overland Park, KS 66211
1/888/888-7696
www.leatherspublishing.com

Acknowledgments

I would like to thank the following loved ones in my life for believing in me and encouraging me to follow my life-long dream to become a writer. Without all of you, none of this would be possible; Richard, my husband, my companion, my confidante, thank you for listening to all of my pipedreams and helping to turn them into reality … thanks for being my first customer! To my children, Pamala, Azadia, and Keenan, thank you for being in my life and making life worthwhile, you three have truly inspired me for life — and future characters; Pamela, my mother, thank you for having me and passing down your gift of gab, creativity, sarcasm and wit, for without you, I would not exist; to Melissa, my sister, and Leslie, my brother, thank you for just being you and being a part of my life; to Curley and Sandra (my adopted parents) for helping me realize one truly can't *live on love*.

A special thank you to Bonnie Swade, my eighth grade English teacher and dear friend, thank you, thank you, for going above and beyond the call of duty, you were the first one who recognized my talent and always encouraged me to write on and fulfill my dream to become a writer – you're not even teaching anymore and you're still grading my papers! Thanks for taking the time out to help me edit.

To anyone I did not mention, who may have given me a piece of advice here and there, a word of encouragement, or just an unknown, but clever remark to inspire a little flavor for one of my characters, thank you.

And last but definitely not least, thanks to my Heavenly Father, for without him none of this nor us would be possible …

"Beware of false prophets, who come to you in sheep's clothing, but inwardly they are ravenous wolves. You will know them by their fruits."
— Matthew 7:15-16
New King James Version

Prologue

I guess you could say we were doomed from the start. I mean, really, how far can a relationship go when your whole family is telling you *No, un-unh, he's all wrong, he's not the one*, and every other negative thing under the sun about your man? And the funniest thing about the whole ordeal is the very thing that attracted me the most about him, repulsed my mother to the highest degree ... his smile. I thought it was the most charming aspect about him; she thought it was the most cunning – and that's putting it mildly.

I was attending a local junior college until I was ready to move onto *bigger and better things* at a four-year university. It was my second year, and I had already been accepted to USC with a partial scholarship, majoring in the Fine Arts division. They had an excellent screenwriting school that I was just dying to get into. My only problem was coming up with the other *part* of the scholarship money. My parents were considered upper middle class – according to the sliding scale – but that meant that it would still be a big blow to their pocket, trying to send me off to a school like that, not to mention assuming additional fees for room and board, books, and any extracurricular activities that I may have wanted to get involved in ... I had no idea what sorority I was going to pledge, but knew that it would be a high priority and had told my parents as much.

So, all that ended up in the wash when Mr. Calvin Jones walked into my life and, literally, swept me off my feet. One day I'm walking down the street, minding my own uncomplicated business, when he appears out of nowhere, riding a raggedy, blue ten-speed, wearing that smile, while pulling the end of my ponytail ... the onset of my complications. You know, looking back on it now, you'd think I would have said, *"Hell, no!"* once I found out that the only thing he owned was that old blue bike. And, I mean *ONLY*. But, of course, stupid me had to make things complicated for myself, and accepted his invitation to a movie. It turns out he did own a car, but I would have actually preferred to ride on the back of his bike, given the option. It was blue, too, but a lot bigger and lot noisier – and I stress the phrase, *a lot*. It had a muffler issue, and some other mechanical situations.

Our first date was a movie at the dollar show, called *Pretty Woman* with Richard Gere and Julia Roberts. Being very brief; it's about a rich, handsome, modern prince who sweeps a common, city girl — with a few minor issues — off her feet, and they fall in love and live happily ever after, yaddah, yaddah, and so forth. Back to *my* story, although I was, by no means, a prostitute, I decided to make this movie work for me, using it as a sign to parallel my destined encounter with Calvin. I thought it meant that we were going to make things happen together and live happily ever after, too. You may be wondering why, since I told you in the beginning that his only assets were himself and an old blue bike. Right, not very much equity, huh? But I forgot to mention that he had told me that he did have money, it just wasn't with him, that he was originally from Hollywood, California, and that his father had money on the way. He had apparently just moved to town a few days prior to our meeting.

Yeah, yeah, yeah, I know already. You're probably asking yourself, why or how did I fall for that one, right? I told you, that was some powerful smile, and he was quite the smooth talker.

Anyhow, one movie date led to another, and then another, until I was completely smitten by the end of one month. Now, keep in mind what it was like for me; some little country, nineteen-year-old bumping into a fine, older – and much worldlier man from Hollywood. Hollywood! You know, Land of the Stars? And as I mentioned earlier, I had always dreamed of being a screenwriter (and secretly, an actress or dancer – or hell, something grand and entertaining!) And in walks — or rides — my ticket to fame, or so I thought. Naturally, it was easy to be star-struck.

After six months of secretly dating, I finally decided it was time I moved out and got my own place. I had tried to win him over with my parents, but to no avail. They were not in the least impressed with his "worldly ways" as they put it, and thought he was a bit too old for me. He was only twenty-three, but I guess that was just old enough to add fuel to the fire. Although I'm sure if he had been some buppie at an Ivy League, they would have graciously excused the age factor.

I continued to go to school but barely finished, what with Calvin always insisting on showing me everything I'd been missing, at local bars and night clubs. He could really dance, and between staying out all night, getting our groove on, and then trying to cram for exams at the crack of dawn, it began to take its toll on my system. I graduated, nonetheless, with an Associate of Arts degree in English and a minor in Spanish. I would be postponing my plans at a university for the time being, but figured that I could always get a job with the school district as a substitute teacher, so all was not completely lost.

It was a very winded romance, and I was happier than I had ever been in my whole life, despite my parents' disapproval. Unbeknownst to them, Calvin was quite the

Casanova, always surprising me with flowers and candy, making spontaneous dinner reservations, and running bath water with the works ... bubbles, candles, rose petals and, of course, some slow jam playing in the background. After a year of all of that pampering, I wasn't surprised when I missed my period ...

Chapter One

I SHOULD HAVE caught on to the first clue of doom when he was late picking us up from the hospital. Twenty-four hours late. I had arrived on Thursday night, had the baby the following morning, and it was now Sunday. Fortunately, I had good medical insurance from my job, which allowed for extended stay – "*should complications arise.*" Well, under the circumstances, they arose. Or at least my blood pressure did.

He finally showed up with a dozen red roses and a half-dozen baby blue roses for our son, Calvin Lee Jones, Jr. Yes, Junior. Something I had always wanted to do, when I had a son, was to name him after his father. Something I would come to regret later in life.

We had argued over the name for months. He said he didn't believe in burdening newborn sons with the same namesake as their fathers. He said it wasn't fair to the sons, and that every man should grow up with his own identity, and not have to worry about living in the shadows or footsteps of his father, especially if he carried the same name. And for once, my mother was in agreement with Calvin, but, of course, for different reasons. Her reasoning was that I should never name a child after his father in case things didn't work out. She said it was bad enough I'd have to look at the child and be reminded anyway of his father, but why go through the burden of having to still call his name after he was gone? I guess she did have a point, but nonetheless, I had won both arguments. One of many things I wish I hadn't done. When I asked him where he had been, all of his attention went, conveniently, to the baby.

"Hey, C.J. How's Daddy's little man?" He proceeded to take him out of my arms, but I fanned him off and finished dressing C.J. in his going-home outfit. It was a powder blue and white striped jumper with yellow elephants dancing across his chest. There were little blue booties to match.

"Calvin, stop! You see me trying to dress him. And don't change the subject on me. You know I hate it when you do that. We were supposed to go home *yesterday*. Now, what happened to you? And what on earth was more important than coming to get your wife and son?"

"Now, hold up. I told you about that wife shit. We're not married yet. So, quit with all those titles."

"We might as well be," I said, rolling my eyes up at him. "I did just bear your firstborn after nineteen and half hours of labor, you know. I think I'm qualified for a title now."

"Whatever, Jaycee. Let's go." He started toward the door, carrying the flowers and the bags, while I struggled to get the baby strapped in his new car seat. The nurse arrived to help me get in the wheelchair.

"Need some help, hon?" she asked me with a smile, looking down at C.J. with as much pride as if she were the one who gave birth. She was actually a very pretty lady to be so big. She was a good two-hundred pounds — plus. She wore her naturally curly, blonde hair in a loose French roll. Her eyes were hazel. I thought she could have done without the baby blue eye shadow, though, whether it matched her outfit or not. It was a little too bright, and a bit too much – not to mention outdated. *Will they ever get it?* I asked myself.

"No, " I answered myself and her simultaneously, and smiled. "I think I got it."

"You take care of that precious baby, now," she said in a motherly tone, hands positioned as if they were supporting her hips.

"Oh, he'll be just fine," I said, stroking his slick, coal mane.

As the nurse wheeled me down the hall, Calvin appeared from around the corner and politely took over, to my surprise.

"I got it from here, ma'am." We both thanked her as she stood aside, gleaming at us as if we were her own kids.

"Take care," she said. If my eyes weren't fooling me, I'd swear she looked a little misty-eyed.

"What's with her, man?" Calvin mumbled. "She acted like she knew us or somethin'."

"So, some people are just naturally sweet and caring. Is that a crime?" Obviously, I was still a little ticked by his late arrival, and with good reason.

"Look, I'm sorry about bein' late, all right? I got tied up."

"Got tied up doing what, Calvin?" We – excuse me — *I* just had a baby. Coming to get us should have been the only thing on your to-do list — the only thing."

"Look, girl. Don't start with me. I'm here, now. So, what?" We were at a traffic light, and he threw his hands up in the air in an exasperated motion. I just shook my head in retirement and turned to check on the baby. He was sleeping soundly, to my relief, despite all the noise we had been making up front. That would be his position throughout his infant stage; him sleeping through his parents' yelling matches.

* * * * *

When we got home, I walked into what looked like a reincarnated clip from the movie, *Animal House*. Beer cans, glasses and empty pizza boxes were lying all over the floor.

"What the hell?" I was highly irritated. "Calvin, what is all of this shit? Is this why you were late?" Now, he knew he had struck a chord when I began to curse. I always tried really hard not to use profanity, because I believed that it just wasn't always necessary. At this point, it had become necessary. "Well, seeing how you were so late, you should have had plenty of time to clean up. So, why am I coming home to this?" I had already put the baby in his bassinet and started picking up the trash.

"Me and the boys were celebratin' C.J.'s birthday. I came home Friday night after you had him to catch a couple of Z's, and they surprised me. We were up all the rest of the night until Saturday morning. I didn't get no sleep, Jaycee, until after they left, around noon. I slept for nine hours straight. So, by the time I woke up and called for you, they said that you were sleepin', so I asked if you could stay until mornin', so you could get your rest."

"Unh," I grunted, still picking up trash.

"I came up there to see the baby, though. They said he was awake and asked if I wanted to come up and feed him. So, I did." I couldn't believe my ears.

"Yeah, right," I said, rolling my eyes. "You came up and fed the baby? For real?"

"And why does that surprise you? He is my son. Or isn't he?" Strike two. I looked around for something to throw at him, and he ducked around the couch for cover, laughing hysterically. I didn't find his joke in the least bit amusing and stomped off to the bedroom to check on C.J. and lie down myself. I was exhausted. Calvin followed me into the room and jumped on the bed beside me. I rolled over and turned my back on him in utter rage.

"Baby, I was just kiddin'. You know I wasn't serious —"

"That wasn't funny, Calvin!" I still had my back turned, and shrugged his hand from my shoulder. Just then the phone rang. Calvin got up to answer it.

"Hello? Hey, what's up?" He walked out of the room, mumbling into the phone. On his way out, I heard him recalling the time and weight of the baby at birth. "Yeah, man. Seven-nineteen p.m., eight pounds, seven ounces ..." *Dang.* I was very impressed that he had remembered all the statistical details of the baby. Maybe he had gone to the hospital and fed the baby. But, whatever, I was still mad. I loved that boy more than anything in the world, and his comment had really hurt me. More than he even knew. But that was Calvin, always the jokester. Never too serious. To him, everything in life was a game. He claimed his attitude was carved into that frame of thinking from growing up in California. He had to downplay things because they tended to get serious enough on their own.

* * * * *

I remember a story he once told me about an ex-girlfriend he had in his early teens, when he was a member of a gang. Up until I met him, I had no idea what a gang really was or the theory behind the whole concept. *Cripps and Bloods* were not a part of everyday Kansas vocabulary ... or at least not mine. But despite the content and graphics of the whole story, it really turned out to be a romantic tragedy. His girlfriend had been a member of the gang and was killed in a drive-by shooting. Calvin admitted that the bullet had been meant for him. Ever since then, he said that he had never ever wanted to get that serious again with someone, just to lose her. Yes, it may have been only puppy love as some people would call it at that age, but usually that's the best kind of love. Certainly, the most genuine, in my eyes.

Chapter Two

I WOKE UP to a baby crying, profusely, for some kind of recognition or attention, it seemed, and remembered that it was my own. I had no idea what time it was, since the clock on the dresser appeared to be hiding under one of Calvin's numerous piles of clothing that he, casually, loved to leave around the house. But I knew it was late because the room was dark, and the street lights had already come on. I picked up the baby and proceeded into the kitchen to grab one of the ready-made bottles the nurse had sent us home with. Then, I noticed how quiet it was, other than the sounds of the baby. Calvin was nowhere to be found. The clock on the microwave read seven twenty-five. I checked the time of the last call on the caller I.D., which was at three-fifteen. That would have been about the time that I drifted off to sleep after he answered the phone. He must have left right after that.

"Four and a half hours!" I said to the air. Where he could have gone that would require that length of time was beyond me. I tried to contain my resurfacing anger, and focused all of my attention on my new man. His little brown eyes were fixed on me, watching my every expression while he feasted on his formula.

"Hey, boo! How's Mommy's little boy? Hunh?" I turned on the T.V. to break up some of the silence. Even though I had this new joy in my life, I was instantly overwhelmed by a sense of loneliness and abandonment. I couldn't believe that Calvin had left the baby and me alone on our first day home. I didn't understand or care for his actions one bit. I was furious. The phone rang, bringing me out of my silent rage.

"Hello? Hi, Mom! I'm fine, how are you? Oh, he's just fine, eating right now. We both just woke up a minute ago. Why am I answering the phone? Oh, Calvin, he stepped out for a minute to go get some more diapers for the baby. He hasn't been gone that long, Mom. He just left. He'll be right back, don't worry. Sure, he's taking care of us, just fine. Mama, don't start. He's been doing real good. You know, he came up to feed the baby the other night while I was asleep. Um-hmm." Why I felt I had to lie to my mother, I don't know. Well, yes I do. I didn't want to get into it with her for the umpteenth time about Calvin. And admitting that I had just woke up and had no idea where my baby's father was would have sent my mother into overdrive. I did not want to go there with her. I was already mad enough on my own without her adding fuel to the fire.

"No, Mom. I don't need you to come over and help. We're fine. You promised to give us a few days alone with the baby so that we could all get used to each other. We'll be fine, really." I wondered, though, myself. Ever since we found out I was pregnant, I had noticed a progressive change in Calvin. I figured it was to be expected, but it still bothered me from time to time. It didn't seem like the norm with him. Then, again, nothing ever was normal with Calvin Jones.

Instead of staying at home more often, like the usual father-to-be, he had started hanging out with his friends again, until wee hours of the night. I remember blowing up his pager one night, after having a very serious episode of Braxton Hicks.

"What, girl?" That was how he answered a page from his eight-months pregnant girlfriend. I could hear music bumping in the background.

"Where are you? I need you to come home. I'm hurting again."

"Didn't the doctor say that was normal? You are carryin' around extra luggage, you know. It's goin' to hurt every now and then, Jaycee."

"Calvin, can't you just come home? Why do I have to beg you to spend some time with me now. I've been doing that a lot here lately, and it's getting old. I'm tired, and you should be here with me, anyway, without me having to ask."

"Maybe I'm tired of it, too. That's why I'm not there now. All you do is whine and complain. This hurts and that hurts. Wah, wah, wah. Jaycee, I'm tired of all that noise. I need to get away sometimes." Thus was the onset of our legacy of bickering. He finally made it home four hours later, after my contractions had faded away.

Chapter Three

FOUR SEEMED TO be the magic number with him. Usually, somewhere in the vicinity of the fourth hour, he would show back up. It was now seven fifty-eight, and C.J. had drifted back off to sleep. I heard the key in the door. He was cutting it close this time.

"Hey." Ironically, he walked in with a pack of Pampers. They were the wrong size, but diapers nonetheless. I suddenly didn't feel so bad about lying to my mother. I didn't acknowledge him and kept on washing out C.J.'s bottles. "I brought Little Man some diapers.

"He can't wear them. They're too big," I scoffed at him without looking up, and kept cleaning.

"Well, he'll grow into them in no time, won't he?"

"Sure." Although I was itching to ask him where he had been, I didn't even bother wasting my breath. That old record was starting to skip. I decided to try a different tune. "So, are you all ready for your interview tomorrow?" He had been laid off from his construction job three months into my pregnancy and had resorted to doing odd jobs around town, set up by some of his buddies. I had worked clear up to my ninth month, so the little setback hadn't really affected us that much. However, now that I was on maternity leave, I was sure it would begin to take its toll.

"I'm not goin'." He said it so bluntly, as he carelessly tossed the pack of diapers onto the couch. They landed with a thud on the hardwood floor as did my friendly tune.

"What do you mean you're not going?" I demanded.

"One of my boys hooked me up with a better gig." *Gigs,* he called them. Jobs didn't come easy in Olathe, Kansas. At least not decent ones – and especially not for a black man. In my eyes and upbringing, a good job was the lifeline of survival in the world. Behind Calvin's dark shades, a job was merely a *gig*, just something to do until something else with more *Benjamins*, as he called it, and more excitement came along.

Just before I had left for vacation, I had talked to one of my co-workers about lining up a stable job for Calvin while I was off. She had talked to her husband for me who was a manager for a distribution company for beverage products. He had graciously set up an interview for Calvin, where he would temporarily be placed on the receiving docks. It sounded like hard work, a change from what Calvin was used to, but it would be decent money coming in, and they allowed overtime. Now, to my dismay and humiliation, I would have to call her and make up an excuse as to why he would not be coming. I was thinking of what I would say to her because I didn't want to jeopardize getting help from her husband again in the future. I wanted to make sure that Calvin always had something to fall back on, if needed. Even when it was crystal clear that he was only thinking of himself, I always had his back. I couldn't believe he was messing things up for us again.

"So, tell me more about this *gig*," I said, sarcastically. "How much does it pay? Does it pay more than eleven-fifty an hour? You know, because the other one *does*. Does it have benefits? Did you forget we just had a baby —"

"Man, shut up! And quit remindin' me that we just had a baby. I am fully aware of that, okay?"

"Well, you're not acting like it," I shot back.

"I'm actin' like my own man who can take care of hisself and find his own jobs, okay? I don't need you runnin' around helpin' me all the time. You're not my damn mama, okay. You got a son now, so that's all you need to be worryin' about. Just mind ya business and let me handle things for a change. Let me be the man of the house." He pounded his chest indignantly.

"Calvin, every time I let you be the man of the house, it seems like we get into more trouble. I'm not trying to be your mother. I'm just trying to help. This isn't just your life anymore, you know. There's me and C.J. to think about, too. And that was a good job. It's still a good job. You could make something out of it, if you just work hard."

"Oh, so now I don't work hard enough? You act like you the only one that's been payin' bills around here."

"I didn't say that. But since you brought it up, I have been footing everything for the past three months or longer. Even before you got laid off, you were spending all of your money on bars, booze and weed, and God knows what else."

To that, he didn't say anything, and I knew I had hit a high note. Whenever he didn't respond to something that I had said, it was sure to be the truth, whether he admitted to it or not. Instead, he brushed past me in the kitchen and reached for a bag of chips from the cabinet, grabbed a beer from the refrigerator, and made himself comfortable on the couch with the remote control. That was typical behavior during one of our infamous feuds. Naturally, I followed him into the living room, demanding feedback. Whether it was positive or negative, it didn't matter, so long as I got a response.

"Calvin?"

"What?" he answered without looking up from the TV.

A mouth full of chips muffled his irritable tone, yet I could still detect it.

"I was asking you about your new job description. What does it entail?"

"What?" Even in the midst of an argument he could amuse me with one of his dumb looks he always gave when I said something out of his vocabulary.

Sometimes I forgot that even though he was a few years older than me, four to be exact, I still overpowered him with my somewhat broader education. Keep in mind that I was contemplating going on to a four-year university when Mr. Jones wheeled into my life, as fate would have it. This was also a big factor as to why my parents hated him so much. They were convinced that he was Lucifer in the flesh, cast upon the earth to steal their daughter's soul.

"Excuse me. What I meant was, what are you going to be doing?"

"I'm a delivery man for Mr. Rawlins. I get a truck and everything. Free gas, pager, the works."

"And just what are you delivering, Calvin?"

"Shit, I don't care when it's payin' me fifty dollars a pop. And I average about ten runs a day. So, you see? I don't need your little slave-drivin' job, when I can make a week's worth in one day, shit, one hour if I want to."

"Calvin, are you dealing drugs? Because that's what it sounds like, and if you are, I don't want any part of it."

"And what does that mean, Jaycee? What, you don't want a nicer car when you've been complainin' for, I don't know how long, about the one you got? You don't want C.J. in the finest gear?"

"He's a baby, what does he know or care about *gear*? As long as he has the essentials. We don't need anything that's bought with drug money. How many times do I have to say that? We talked about this, Calvin, when we first met. I thought you were done with that life."

"Baby, I'm never done with where I came from. It's who I am. This is a survival of the fittest world. You know the deal. You gotta get in where you fit in. How many times have I told you that? I'm a father now. Playtime is over. It's time to step up and come up. You know what I'm sayin', Jay? I want the same things you want for him. But we not gonna get it if we settle for less." I hated it when he called me Jay. Whenever he shortened my name, it meant that he was serious about something. Him being serious on this subject really worried me. His intentions were good, as always for the majority of the time, but his direction was all bad.

"A good, *stable* job is settling for less?"

"Yeah, when I can get *more* this way, not to mention faster."

"More, faster. Is that how you want our son to grow up, Calvin? Getting things the fast and easy way?"

"Now, you know I don't. That's why I'm doin' it for him, now, so he won't have to. At this rate, with the money I'll be makin', we'll have plenty left to start savin' for his college fund."

"Oh, no we won't. We're not going to let some low-life drug dealer send our son to college. My God, Calvin. What has gotten into you? What happened to our pact we made, to do things together the right way, the *honest* way? You said you were done with that life, because it doesn't get you anywhere but in trouble, remember? Well, what happened to all that talk?"

"All that talk was just that, Jaycee. Talk. Talk can't keep the bills paid. Talk can't keep you in nice things like fine clothes and real gold. Talk can't get us up out of this little dinky ass apartment, and into your dream house you keep *talkin'* about."

"Well, talk's been doing fine so far. The bills are paid.

I made sure of that before I went on maternity leave, remember?" Now, I was just talking, and he knew that. Sure, I had paid the bills up for awhile. But we both knew that time was running out, and, eventually everything would be due again before I was due back at work.

I had asked for an extended maternity leave, which meant that I was off for a total of three months instead of the average six weeks. It was my first baby, and I had wanted as much time as possible before I handed him off to strangers for eight hours a day, licensed or not. I had asked my mother to babysit, but my father had stepped in and forbade her to. Ever since I had moved out of the house and in with Calvin, my father and I had been on not-so-good terms. He had sworn that Calvin Jones would be the death of me, as did everyone. But Mom had softened up after she learned of my pregnancy. I wasn't sure if it was out of pity for me starting a family so young, or just genuine, unconditional love, but I had invited the change, nonetheless. And secretly, she had told me that she would have loved to watch C.J. for me, but I had understood why she couldn't. No one liked to make waves with my father, although I had always managed to create a ripple or two from time to time.

* * * * *

"Now that we're on the subject. That's another reason why I took this job. I don't want you to go back to work. You won't have to, with the Benjamins I'll be bringin' in." I couldn't believe my ears.

"What?! You've got to be joking. Do you honestly think that that type of money has any longevity? Come on, Calvin. You know better than that. You know that job is not going to last. That type of money never lasts. That type of life doesn't last. I've heard all about it from you, the horse's mouth. That's why I can't believe what I'm hearing. What is wrong with you? Why are you letting yourself get sucked back in?"

"I'm not gettin' sucked back into nothin', Jaycee. I'm steppin' up like a man, like I'm supposed to."

"Risking your life and all that we have here together is not my idea of being a man."

"And what is your idea, Jaycee? Hunh? What's a man to you? Bustin' his ass for twelve or thirteen hours a day for a little paycheck that takes two weeks to cover all the bills — if that? Then comin' home, so tired and beat that he can't even make love to you, 'cause he only got a good four or five hours to get some sleep before the next day?"

"It's not all about that. You're just minimizing everything."

"Oh, am I? Well, try to minimize this." He reached down in his pocket and pulled out a wad of hundred dollar bills and casually tossed it on the coffee table. There were also fifties and twenties in the bunch. The wad unfolded from the pressure of the throw and money went everywhere, spilling onto the floor. I picked up the loose bills and began counting, in shock. I had never seen so much money at one time in my life, other than at a bank.

"One hundred, two hundred, three hundred, four hundred, five hundred, twenty, forty, sixty, eighty, five-hundred eighty, six hundred, seven hundred, eight, nine, one thousand, two thousand —" And that was just a portion of what I had picked up off of the floor. I dropped the money just as quickly as I had picked it up and stepped back as if it was a fire that had spread out of control. "Calvin, how much money is here?"

"Enough, for now." He gathered the money back up and took all but five hundred dollars out of my hand. "You can keep the change, baby. Go buy some stuff for our son. Oh, and yourself, too." I threw the money back at him.

"You can keep your dirty money. I don't want any part of it." I brushed past him and went to check on the baby. As soon as I did it, I questioned myself. That was a lot of money. But then another voice entered my mind and assured me that I did the right thing. Yes, it was a lot of money, but like my grandmother always said, "*All money ain't good money.*" So I held on to that thought, and prayed that it would keep me.

Chapter Four

I HAD BEEN doing a lot of praying since I first found out that I was pregnant. First, I had asked God for forgiveness, for breaking the rules of sex outside of marriage. Of course, we (*we*, being unwed mothers) all tend to repent *after* the fact when faced with such conditions. Then I asked Him to make me a good mother, and Calvin a good father. And, of course, I asked Him to bring me a healthy baby. And if those three wishes were granted, especially the last one, I had promised to attend church more regularly, with or without Calvin. Funny, how He loves us unconditionally, yet we tend to pray with wagers, always based on certain terms and conditions. You know what I mean? *God, if you do this, I'll do that. God, if you fix this, I'll work on that.* Yaddah, yaddah. I had to find out the hard way that it doesn't work like that. Oh, He works, most mysteriously, but by His terms, not ours.

* * * * *

Three weeks had gone by, and Calvin and I were still arguing about the money.

"Girl, what's wrong with you? Why don't you keep the money? Money is money, baby. Shit, it don't matter where it comes from. It all spends the same."

"It's the principle, Calvin. I know and *you* know where it comes from, and that's all that matters."

"Oh, there you go with that goody two shoes talk, again. You know, you need to quit trippin' all the time, and live a little. Quit worryin' about bein' good all the time. You really think that stuff matters when it all boils down? When it's your time, it's your time, no matter where you at or what you doin'. How many times I gotta tell you that?"

I hated it when he tried to argue me down on something he was clearly wrong about. So, he was an expert when it came to topics about street life and drugs, and so forth, but religion was clearly not his forté. He didn't even go to church, and had claimed to be agnostic. Meaning, he wasn't exactly an atheist, but he wasn't quite a true believer, either. God forbid, had my parents ever found out. No pun intended. We had talked about that during our courtship, also. And I really should have taken heed to that obvious red light. But like a fool, I thought I could change his viewpoint, in time. My first of many mistakes.

"And how many times do I have to tell you that it does matter, Calvin? Whether you choose to believe it or not, there is a Heaven and Hell, and your actions determine where you will go." I had changed the baby and handed him to Calvin, so I could go warm up a fresh bottle.

Calvin just shook his head and laughed at me, looking down at C.J. "Your mama is somethin' else, boy. You'd think she was Mother Theresa or somebody."

I came back with the bottle and took C.J. back. "Well, since we're on the subject, when are we getting married? You said we would after the baby came. We are living in sin, you know, and God don't like ugly." I was joking with him now, although he didn't know it. I had just wanted to get him back for the little remark he had made about me being Mother Theresa.

"Now, here we go. You're just never satisfied, are you? You just can't leave well enough alone." Calvin sighed with exasperation and rose from the bed. He walked away, shaking his head in defeat. Clearly, I had tapped another nerve on that topic.

"Good," I thought. *"Maybe if I bug him long, enough he'll give in. And if that doesn't work, I'll threaten to leave him — with C.J."* I smiled down at C.J. as I rocked him back to sleep. "Surely, he'll have to give in and marry me, now that you're here," I assured myself. I heard Calvin's pager go off, as I was laying C.J. down in his crib.

"Now, where is he going?" I demanded of the air. I stomped off toward the front room, hoping to catch him in the driveway, as I raced to the front door, but to no avail. *"Ass!"* I pouted. He had already taken off, that fast. He hadn't even taken the time to call the number back, which really made me irritable, not to mention inquisitive.

I slammed the door and flung myself on the couch in utter disgust, matched with fatigue. I didn't know who was wearing me down more, Calvin or Calvin, Jr. I was beginning to feel like a baton being passed between them in a race for my attention. I couldn't grasp the concept of Calvin's recent flightiness for the life of me.

* * * * *

Just the other day, we had finally sat down, civilly, and talked about his new job, and his so-called duties. He had promised that it wouldn't be an ongoing task, that he felt it was necessary for the time being until I went back to work. Yes, I had ultimately convinced him into letting me go back to work. I had really tried to understand his viewpoint on doing what you have to do in order to survive, and under the circumstances, felt I had no valid comeback, so I had agreed to his terms — for the time being. But what I couldn't understand was his progressive distance from home. He was away on deliveries more frequently than before and for longer periods of time. If you can believe it, he was supposed to have a nine-to-five job, because this Mr. Rawlins character had enough *staff* at night. And I had demanded his weekends be off limits for me and the baby. He had agreed to compromise with my requests, and asked his boss if he could be on call.

Chapter Five

THE PHONE RANG, and it was my mother again. Damn, she had impeccable timing.

"Jaycee?"

"Hi, Mom."

"How are you doing, and how's the baby?"

"Fine and fine."

"And why do you keep answering the phone? You're supposed to be resting."

"Well, Mom, you keep calling." As soon as I said that, I knew I had messed up.

"I know you're not getting smart with me, missy — and just what do you mean by that?"

"Nothing, Mom. Sorry. I didn't mean it like that. It's just that, never mind." I really was not in the mood for any further debate, especially with my mother.

"Where is Calvin? And why isn't he answering the phone so you can rest?"

"He's here, Mom. He's in the shower." Yes, I was doing it again, lying through my pretty little straight (from four years of braces) teeth.

"Un-hunh. Well, you tell him I said to turn the ringer off and let the answering machine pick up the messages so you can get some rest. You know, you can't take care of that baby properly if you're not taking care of yourself."

"I know, Mother. I'll be fine. I was just getting ready

to take a nap when you called."

"Oh, well, I'll let you go. I was just checking in on my grandson. You know, no matter what your father says, he's still my flesh and blood, my first grandchild, and I love him —" her voice started to crack, and I thought I was going to die, right there, as my eyes started to water. "I love you, Jaycee Leanne."

"I love you, too, Mama." I hung up and balled into the sofa pillow. I cried so hard, I put myself to sleep, just like a baby.

* * * * *

"Jay? Jay? Baby, wake up. We need to talk." Calvin was shaking me lightly on my shoulder. I sat up, rubbing my eyes, a little disoriented from the nap.

"What? What time is it?" I asked, looking at my watch. It read four twenty-six. I had slept for three hours straight. "Oh, my God," I exclaimed, panicking. I couldn't believe that I had slept that long and hard, without the baby waking up. "I need to go check on C.J." Calvin took my hand lightly, holding me down.

"Just relax. The baby's fine. I just laid him back down. I've been home for awhile. I came in and saw you sleepin', so I kept quiet. He only woke up for a minute, and when I picked him up to hold him, he went back to sleep."

"Did you try to give him a bottle?"

"I told you, he went back to sleep."

"Well, I should probably wake him up for a bottle. He hasn't eaten in four hours —"

"Let the boy sleep, Jay. He'll be okay. He'll wake up when he's hungry. Besides, it'll give us some time to talk."

"About what?" I asked, suspiciously. I noticed he had taken quite a serious tone all of a sudden, which really disturbed me.

"About this," he reached in his pants pocket and pulled out a little burgundy box. My heart skipped a beat or two.

"Wha-what's that?" I asked, a bit shocked. "Is that what I think it is, because if it's not, Calvin, I don't think that's very funny — in the least. I'm not up for your little practical jokes. I'm very tired, you know —"

"Man, you talk too much! Can you stop raggin' long enough to see what's in the box?" He had appeared to be irritated, but I could see a smile forming out of the corner of his mouth. I took the box from him and opened it. I was speechless, as I looked down at a half-carat diamond and gold engagement ring. It was huge! Not to mention, breathtaking. I had never in my life seen a prettier ring. It was something to feast your eyes upon. I sat there gawking at it for God knows how long until Calvin awoke me from my trance. "Well, are you gonna try it on or not?"

"Oh," I said, still in a daze. "Yes."

"Here, allow me." He took the box from me and gently held my hand as he slid the ring on my finger. It was the closest, gentleman-like gesture that he had ever made toward me. I was truly stunned and quite impressed with my new fixture. I made a mental note to go have my nails done the following week. With a ring like that, you couldn't half-step with Lee Press-Ons.

"Calvin, is this real? It's gorgeous!" I could finally talk, as I held my hand up in speculation, moving it back and forth to catch the light.

"Hell, yeah, it's real! And you're welcome."

"Oh, thank you, baby," I said, giving him a big bear hug. "I'm sorry. It's just so big."

"So, when you wanna do this thing?" he asked, losing his gentleman status. Now, that sounded like the Calvin I knew. I rolled my eyes at him, as I got up to look at the calendar in the kitchen. He followed me and wrapped his arms around me, his head hanging over my shoulders, as we looked together at the dates. We started running our fingers together across the numbers, and we both stopped on the fourteenth, simultaneously. We were in the month of February, and just three days away from Valentine's Day, which sounded perfect for a romantic elopement. I marveled at our twin-like thoughts, which we had every now and then, when we weren't fighting. But then my mind started fluttering, as I thought of my parents and friends and all of the other millions of details that a first-time bride thinks of when she imagines the more traditional, planned wedding, and I sighed in bewilderment.

"What's wrong, Jay?"

"Well, the fourteenth sounds perfect because it's Valentine's Day, and everything, but —"

"But what?"

"Well, don't you think it's a little hasty? I mean, what about our parents, and my friends — and your friends? I would want to invite all of them. I mean, it is the first time for both of us. Maybe we should do it right and have a traditional ceremony, where everyone we care about is there to celebrate with us. And my mother would be horrified anyway if I just ran out and got married without her knowing — not to mention what my father would think."

"Well, aren't they gonna be *horrified* no matter what? Did you forget that your parents don't like me?"

Oh, yeah, I said to myself, snapping back to reality. There was the matter of the ongoing feud between Calvin and my parents. What was I thinking? They would not be happy about the news, not in the least.

"Well, they'll just have to get used to the idea, won't they?" I reassured Calvin and myself at the same time.

"Besides," said Calvin, "I'm okay with the elope part.

I, uhh, already did the big wedding thing. It's not all that." If I was white, I'd swear that my ears turned bright red at the sound of that news. He had casually slinked away from me and was back over on the couch, swinging his legs over the armrest. I spun around and glared at him.

"What did you just say?"

"I said, I already did the big wedding —"

"Yeah, I heard that. But what did you mean by it? What do you mean, you already did the big wedding thing? You mean to tell me that you've already been married before?"

"Yeah," he replied, scratching his head. I could not believe what I was hearing.

"And why haven't you told me this before, Calvin? What were you thinking?"

"I don't like to talk about it. And it's really not all that big a deal. It didn't even last." I calmed down a couple of degrees when he said that, thinking of the story he had told me about his girlfriend that was killed.

"Oh? Were you married to Cynthia?" That was her name.

"No. It was somebody else, after her." I was starting to feel like a malfunctioned thermometer, as the heat rose again to my temples. I was in total shock. I was so mad I couldn't even talk. I just stood there in the kitchen, leaning against the counter with my arms folded.

"I just did it to get my mind off Cindy."

Cindy. I don't know why, but him calling her by her nickname seemed to bother me, even in her death.

"It was just one of those rebound things, you know. She was just real nice, and was there for me after all of that happened. But after six months I got tired of her, she got tired of me, and we both went our separate ways, and had the whole thing annulled. So, you see, it's nothin' to trip about." He looked at me with those pleading brown eyes. And then he smiled and walked over to me, taking me into his arms. He held on to me as if his life depended on it. He often hugged me when I was mad at him, and I hated him for it, because it always seemed to work. It amazed me how he always knew what buttons to push with me when he needed to win me over. Call it corny all you want, but whenever he touched me, I would truly feel an electric current go through me. That's how bad I loved him.

"I'm sorry for not telling you about all that sooner. It was over and done so fast, I don't really consider it a part of my life, so I tend to block it out at times."

"So, why did you decide to tell me now?" I asked.

"I don't know. You started carryin' on about *our first wedding* and all that, and I thought it would make things easier on the both of us if you knew it wasn't mine. That way, we won't have to go through all those changes with a bunch of unnecessary plannin'. And anyway, it's not the weddin' that makes the marriage, it's the couple."

Boy, he was good, wasn't he? "All that other stuff is material — and a waste of money, if you ask me. Besides, wouldn't you rather have more money for the honeymoon? That's really the most important part." Well, he did have a point there.

"I guess you're right. The honeymoon is supposed to be pretty special. And since my parents aren't going to be too gung-ho about all of this, they probably won't be helping with the expenses —"

"You better believe they won't. But, baby, don't worry about that. I got it all covered. He let go of me and went to retrieve something from his leather coat, hanging in the closet by the front door. It looked like a bunch of pamphlets or something. "We'll just spend all of our money on the honeymoon and I'll take you anywhere you wanna go. You pick." He spread them out all over the coffee table, and lay back on the couch with his hands folded behind his head. There were traveling brochures, full of colorful pictures of different beach resorts. I felt like a little girl in a candy store. There was Hawaii, Jamaica, Cancun, and for whatever reason, he had even thrown in a couple of brochures on ski resorts.

"What is this, Calvin? You know I don't ski!" I exclaimed, rolling my eyes up at him. He started laughing.

"I know. I just wanted you to have a little variety to pick from."

"Uh-huh," I said.

"Besides, I can teach you."

"Teach me what?"

"How to ski," he said.

"What? Get out of here! How do you know how to ski, and you're from California?"

"I went once with some of my little white friends in high school, on Spring Break."

"I thought most people go somewhere summery on Spring Break. Isn't that the whole point of having the vacation, to go somewhere hot and fun?"

"Not when you already live around sun and beaches, twenty-four seven." I raised my eyebrows, and nodded my head in agreement.

"I guess you have a point there." I focused my attention back on the brochures.

"Well, how about Cancun? It would be nice to use some of my Spanish. I'd like to think I didn't study it all of those years for nothing."

"I didn't know you could talk Spanish."

"Ah, si, mi hombre. Me te amo mucho! Te amo con mi corazon totalmente! Te quiero mi esposo por el resto mi la vida." By now, I had pinned him down on the couch, straddling his body in a wrestler's position, my knees touching his armpits, my hands seductively cuffing his wrists.

"Hey, now. Slow your roll, baby. Save some of that for the honeymoon," he said, chuckling with a boyish, almost shy grin. "And what were you sayin' anyway? That sounded kind of good, whatever it was."

"I said, yes, my man. I love you very much. I love you with all my heart, and that I want you to be my husband forever."

"Where did you learn all that Spanish? You should be one of them bi-language people. Don't they make a lot of money?"

I laughed at his ignorance and sat up. God, he could be so stupid at times. Cute, but stupid.

"The word is bilingual, honey. I learned it in school. And, yes, they do make pretty good money. But I'm a little rusty — actually a lot rusty. I don't know it as well as I sound. I just know the basics really good. When you're a bilinguist, you have to know a lot more than that. I mean, it can get really technical, and a lot of the foreigners speak slang just like we do in English, and those words aren't taught in school. So you have to really be up on your verbage. I've thought about it, but I'd have go back to school and get my degree, and all that. And with C.J. now, who has time?"

"We could get a babysitter and you could go back to school?"

I looked at him like he was crazy. I couldn't believe my ears. Mr. High School Dropout was telling me to go back to school. Imagine that. He must have been reading my mind. "Now, I know you thinkin' I ain't got no business tellin' you what to do about your edjumuhcashun …"

"Shut up, Calvin!"

"Naw, really. I feel bad about pullin' you out of school and all. And I know that's one of the reasons why your folks hate me so much. So, they would probably really like it if you went back. And maybe they would get around to likin' me more if I helped pay for it."

"First of all, Calvin, you did not pull me out of anything. I was getting bored with the whole thing anyway. I shouldn't have gone off to college straight out of high school in the first place. That's probably why I got burned out so fast. But I did finish two whole years, so it's okay. It's not like I never went at all. I have enough under my belt to still get a decent job. We'll be fine, as long as we have each other," I said, hugging him. "Besides, I'll go back to school when you go back." He shoved me away, lightly.

"See, there you go, always startin' somethin'. The subject was you – not me. You couldn't pay me to go back to school. Shit, you must be crazy!" I knew that was a lost cause. I had just wanted to get a rise out of him, just for kicks. It had worked.

"Just crazy in love with you," I said, getting up to go check on the baby. It was near time for his next feeding.

Chapter Six

WE WOKE UP to someone pounding violently on the door. I sat up in the bed and looked at the clock on the nightstand. It was Sunday, and only 5:30 in the morning. Who could be visiting at this hour was beyond me, but I had a funny feeling that they weren't wanting coffee and donuts.

"Calvin, we know you're in there, you little motherfucker! Answer the door!" I hated, I was right. Calvin had already jumped up out of the bed and was putting on clothes. He seemed to be scrambling for something underneath the bed. Whatever he was looking for, I wished he would hurry up and find it because I didn't know how much longer that door was going to hold up. And the baby was starting to squirm in his crib.

"Calvin! Who is that? And what do they want?"

"Just be quiet, and stay in here. I'll be back. He finally rose from the floor with his house shoes in his hands and proceeded to the front room to answer the door. I shook my head in disbelief. Some strange men were beating at our door, probably armed with guns or something, and here he was worried about what was on his feet, as if he were just going out to the front lawn to get the Sunday paper.

As soon as Calvin had unlocked the dead bolt, I could hear the men rushing in, like a tidal wave. It sounded like they had just turned over the coffee table or maybe threw Calvin on top of the coffee table. I wasn't for sure, but the noise was very breaking and ultimately woke up the baby. He began crying and I rushed to comfort him.

"Where's my money, you little bitch?! I want it, and I want it now."

Suddenly, I recognized the voice. It was Mr. Rawlins, Calvin's boss. I had spoken to him a couple of times on the phone, regarding Calvin's whereabouts. Seemed like I wasn't the only one who couldn't track him down on occasion. I carefully peeked out of our bedroom door. Calvin was arched back on the couch, holding his hands up as a shield. Mr. Rawlins was doing all of the talking, but another man, whom I didn't recognize, was doing his dirty work for him, holding a gun up to my fiancee's head. Not thinking, I ran out of the bedroom with the baby and started yelling at both of the men.

"Leave him alone! What do you want? Get out of my house!"

"Jaycee, get out of here," yelled Calvin. "I told you to stay in the room! Get my son out of here!"

"Ma'am, this is none of your business. You better listen to him and leave us to settle this. That baby don't need to see this." That was the voice of Mr. Rawlins, the boss man. I don't know what got into me at that moment. It was either shock from utter fear or just plain stupidity, but I walked right up to him and gave him a piece of my mind.

"Mister, you've got some nerve to come up in my house, flashing guns around at my fiancée, then telling me what's an appropriate environment for my son. If you're so concerned about his welfare, why are you here like this, causing such a disruption?"

"Because your little boyfriend, here, owes me some money and I'm here to collect. Now, I don't mean no disrespect, ma'am. I just want what's mine. Nobody fucks with my money." He forgot about me and focused his eyes back on Calvin. "So, we can do this nice and simple, or we can get ugly. The choice is yours. Now, you either hand over the money, or give me back my dope."

We were all standing there, waiting for Calvin to make his decision. Just when I was about to make it for him, he started talking.

"I don't have it right now, but give me a few hours, man. Please? It's six o'clock now. I swear, I'll have it to you by six p.m. tonight."

Mr. Rawlins stepped back and motioned for his gunman to withdraw his stance.

"Okay. You go get me my money. And I mean, if you don't have it to me by six o'clock on the fuckin' D.O.T., your ass is mine. And just for a little insurance …" he turned and looked at me. "I'm gonna need that ring back, ma'am." I gasped and covered my hand in defense, while still holding the baby.

"No," I started crying, "you can't take my engagement ring."

"I'm sorry to have to do this to you, but I know that it was bought with my money. When your boyfriend here returns my money, I'll think about givin' it back."

"Baby, just give him the ring. I'll buy you another one just like it. I promise," said Calvin.

I looked at him in disgust, took off my ring and threw it down. It bounced off of the coffee table and landed on the floor, right by Mr. Rawlins' feet. He was wearing black, leather boots. They were so shiny, you could see the reflection of the ring. I ran into the bedroom with the baby and slammed the door. He started crying and I cried with him. There was a half-bottle of formula sitting on the nightstand. I fed it to him and he eventually fell back asleep. I held him close to me and we both fell asleep.

※ ※ ※ ※ ※

I woke up and found Calvin packing. I must have really been in a deep sleep, because I noticed that C.J. was back in his crib. Calvin must have put him there while I was sleeping.

"What are you doing, Calvin?"

"What's it look like I'm doin'? I'm packin' up our shit. Jaycee, we have to get up outta here — now. I thought I'd let you rest awhile, after this mornin' and all. But now I need your help." He stopped packing and knelt down in front of me while I sat upright on the bed. He took my hands in his. "Baby. It's time to make that move."

"What are you talking …"

"Hush now, and listen to me. We ain't got much time. We gotta leave town today. If we leave now, we can be still be married by tomorrow, just like we planned."

"But, Calvin …"

"Don't worry about a thing, baby. I've got it all planned out." He stood up and walked back around to the other side of the bed. He bent down again and went underneath the bed in the same spot he had gone to earlier this morning when our unexpected guests had shown up. He pulled out a suitcase and unzipped it.

What came next, you wouldn't believe it if you had seen it with your own two eyes. Carefully arranged in orderly stacks lay crisp, clean, green dollar bills. And I don't mean George Washingtons. The money I had seen the other day was nothing compared to this. All I could do was sit there in awe, with my mouth open. I was speechless — a mere mute! I watched Calvin run his hands over the top layer. He caressed it like someone would after they had just waxed and polished their brand new car, very carefully so as not to leave fingerprints. He had the biggest smile on his face like he had just found a pot of gold. I guess you could say it was a pot of gold, but whether he had found it or not was highly debatable.

My jaws finally loosened up enough to allow me to close my mouth, and I swallowed the lump of air that had formed in my throat, which had kept me from speaking. "Umm, Calvin? Wh-where did you get all of that money? Please tell me it doesn't belong to Mr. Rawlins — and please, please tell me that you didn't almost get us killed over something that was here all along, that you could've given back!"

"It might've been his money for starters, but it's mine now. All mine. Jaycee, you have to learn some things in life. Sometimes you can't just sit around, waiting for opportunity to knock at your front door. Sometimes you have to do the knockin'. And you know, every now and then, after nobody answers, you might try the door knob. If it's locked and it doesn't turn, then it's not your time just yet. But, you know, every now and again, you might just find that knob that does turn and – wah-lah — the door opens! Now, whoever was careless and forgot to the lock the door, that's on them. It's all up to you whether you're gonna go and find your treasure or pass your opportunity up. The choice is all yours." I looked at him in disbelief and shook my head.

"Calvin, I cannot believe you! You stole that money. That wasn't opportunity, that was theft! You were wrong, and you need to give that money back to its rightful owner. Don't you realize what you're doing? You're putting your life — our lives — in danger! You nearly got us all killed this morning! And for what? Your greed for money — money that's not even yours. And dirty money on top of that —"

"Oh, here we go with that Saint talk again. Girl, how many times do I gotta tell you that there ain't no such thing as clean or dirty money. Money is money. Clean or dirty, it all spends the same, baby. Look…" he closed the suitcase up and continued packing. He checked his watch, and, in sequence I glanced at the clock sitting on the nightstand. It read ten-o-six. "Jaycee, we don't have much time left. Boss Man will be back, like he said, in exactly eight hours. I need you to start packing you and C.J.'s stuff. I don't know what all you wanna take or leave behind. Whatever you leave behind, I can get it back for you, so don't worry about that."

"Calvin, have you not heard a word I've said?" Calvin stopped packing, and came over to me. He took both of my hands in his and looked me dead in the eye.

"Jaycee, a deal of mine went bad the other night. I didn't tell you about it because those kind of things ain't none of your concern. But I'm telling you now, so you can understand. I delivered some bad dope to some people and now they want their money back."

"Okay, so just give them their money back. What's the big deal?" I asked.

"The big deal is I don't have the money to give back because it's already spent. How do you think you got that ring?" I looked down at my bare finger. "And I went to Boss Man about it for help, and he wouldn't help me. He didn't believe me and accused me of tamperin' with the dope myself. So, I figure, he's gonna leave my ass out like that, then fuck him. Yeah, I took the money, to get him back. I got enough to pay those people back, because they're Italians, baby. And you don't fuck with Italians, 'cause they got Mafia connections and shit. But I also got a little extra for us to get away on. I figure we can be on a plane to Acapulco in a couple of hours. You game?"

The phone rang and saved me from answering him right away. We both just stood there, looking at it, afraid to answer it. We decided to let the answering machine pick it up.

"Hi, baby." It was my mother. Didn't I say she had impeccable timing? "It's your Mama. Are you there? Well, good, then you must be resting like I told you to." I shook my head, half-smiling. Well, I won't keep you, I was just wondering what you were doing tomorrow. Thought you might like to come over for dinner and bring that grandson of mine over for a little visit. You probably could stand a little company with *that boy* working nights and all."

I glanced at Calvin to see his reaction. He looked at me and gave me that smirky, "I ain't payin' her no mind" expression that he always gives on anything involving my mother. "Well, let me know. Love you. Bye."

* * * * *

So many things were whirling through my mind at that moment. I didn't know which way was the right way. Do I run away with Calvin and live happily ever after — but always having to look over my shoulder? Or do I stay right here in what I know is rightfully and honestly mine, and let Calvin go and get caught — or killed — on his own? I felt like I was in one of those cartoons or sitcoms where you have the angel sitting on one shoulder and the devil lounging on the other, and they're both trying to persuade you to side with them. Oh, of course, I knew what was really right, but when you're in love — I mean really head over heels, in that stupid phase of love, your mind plays tricks on you and makes you think and do things that you wouldn't normally fathom.

* * * * *

"Jaycee? You hear me?" I broke from my stupor at the sound of Calvin's voice. "So, you in this with me or not, baby?" I looked over at C.J. for one more ounce of justification for staying or leaving, and then I finally answered Calvin.

"Yeah, baby. I'll go with you."

Suddenly, a big, boyish grin spread across his face in what looked like relief, as he walked over and hugged me. I really believe he had been worried that I would say no.

"That's my girl. I knew I could count on you." Of course, he could, always. But the doubt was my being able to count on him. And was that money really the answer to all my prayers and concerns with Calvin? I was soon about to find out.

"Calvin, before we leave, I have to go see my parents —"

"No, Jaycee. Out of the question. We can't risk that. What if Boss Man knows where they live? And he probably has someone watchin' us anyway."

"Wait a minute. What do you mean 'out of the question'? I wasn't *asking* you could I go see them, I was telling you that I want to go say goodbye. I can't just vamp out on them like that — they're my parents. They haven't even spent time with their grandson yet, and we're talking about leaving the country. And if he has someone watching us, how do you expect us to get out of this apartment and onto a plane without any problems? Did you go steal a magic carpet, too?"

He shot me one of those looks he often gave when we were arguing, and I had outwitted him with some sly remark. It was a look of utter annoyance.

Any other time I would be amused by my own sarcasm, but this was no time for games, and I wasn't playing. I was serious about going to see my family because I wasn't sure when the next time would be — or if there even would be a next time. And I had thought about maybe leaving the baby behind with my parents, making them think that we were just going away for a couple of weeks on our honeymoon. But then I remembered that I hadn't even told them that we were getting married. *Oh, yeah,* I thought. *I had forgotten that small detail. Okay, so I'd just tell them that his mother was sick, and we were going to California for a couple of days to see about her, that maybe seeing her new grandson would cheer her up.* They wouldn't like it, especially my mother, but the lie would work.

"Fine, you go see your Mom and Pops, tell them I said hello, hugs and kisses." I returned his annoyed look, and rolled my eyes. "Then meet me back here in an hour."

"What? Calvin, I may never see my parents again, and all I get is one hour?"

"C'mon, girl. You know this is serious shit we're dealin' with. We don't have much time as it is. We gotta make sure we have enough of a headstart before Boss Man comes back. And I don't doubt he saw all those booklets layin' around in the living room, so when he gets here and sees that we're gone, he'll be on our tails in no time."

"He wasn't paying any attention to those brochures. He was too busy worrying about his money."

"Just because he didn't say anything, don't think he didn't notice. Boss Man scopes everything out, believe me, girl. I wouldn't put it behind him to have somebody already waitin' for us at the airport."

"Calvin, if you're so sure he already knows your every move, then why are we running? I don't understand. You keep talking like you know you're going to get caught, so why bother?" I shook my head in bewilderment. Calvin wasn't making any sense to me, and the more I thought about it, the more confused and scared I became.

"It's all a part of the game, baby. Run 'til you can't run no more. Put up a good fight. You know the deal."

No, I didn't know the deal, but I did know that we

were getting in over our heads, big time. Maybe to the point of no return.

"Look, we're down to six hours," he said, checking his watch again. I looked over at the clock on the nightstand, which read eleven fifty-seven. We had been arguing for two hours straight. I marveled at his sudden gift of time-keeping, and wondered if I had threatened his life, would he had been more prompt about coming home at night. "Forget about meetin' me back here. Let's just finish up here right now, and I'll just drop you off at your parents and come back for you in a couple of hours. Instead of goin' to KCI, we'll just drive to Oklahoma City and catch a flight at the airport there. That should throw them off."

"What about my car? We can't just leave it sitting."

"Remember, I told you I had some family down there, on my mother's side? I'll just call one of my cousins to come get it and park it in their garage until we come back from Acapulco."

"Then what?"

"Then what, what?"

"After we get back from our honeymoon, then where will we go? Where will we live?" Just when I thought I had finally reached my comfort zone — leaving home, owning my own apartment, starting my own family, getting married — just when all of my dreams were finally becoming reality, everything seemed to be going down the drain all at once. I loved Calvin with all of my heart, but I was terrified of running away with him into the unknown and leaving everything behind that was familiar. And what was the money good for, if in the end it cost us our lives?

"I can take you back to California with me or we can stay in Oklahoma, or go wherever you wanna go, baby. It's your world now."

How ironic that sounded, because at that particular

moment, it didn't seem like my world at all — far from it. In my world, I didn't have to run from drug dealers and hitmen, spraying bullets everywhere. In my world, I didn't have to wonder where the next day was going to take me because I already had it mapped out in my dayplanner, just like my Mom.

* * * * *

We finished packing and began loading up the trunk of my car. It was a '90 Honda Civic, so only so much would fit. I hated leaving my furniture. I had tried to talk Calvin into letting me put it in storage, but he thought that it would be too obvious of a move to his boss, so we ended up pawning it to some neighbors upstairs. It was a black sectional with multi-colored feathers imprinted all over, and I had a black and brass entertainment center which held a 27" TV. There was also a coffee table with matching end tables to go along with the ensemble. We were able to sell everything – minus the coffee table, of course — for a little under two hundred dollars. It was a complete rip-off, considering what I had paid, but Calvin had promised that he would replace everything as soon as we were settled.

Chapter Seven

ON THE WAY to my parents' house, we had a close call with Calvin's boss. We drove right past him and his entourage, but they were too busy waiting in a McDonald's drive-thru to notice us. And, just in case they happened to turn their heads our way, Calvin had managed to change lanes and get alongside a Culligan van. I about pissed on myself. If ever there was a death wish relay, we seemed to be the lead contenders, baton in hand.

My inner voice immediately returned to question my judgment once again. *Now, are you sure you want to go through with this?* I asked myself. *Because this is your last chance to back out. Just spill the beans and tell Mom and Dad everything! They'll throw Calvin out, threaten to call the cops, and forbid you to go. What a perfect solution!*

I was startled back into reality by the touch of Calvin's hand. Lately, any little thing gave me the jitters.

"You all right, Jay?"

"Yeah, baby." I smiled in reassurance, and he winked at me. We turned onto the street that my parents lived on, and the closer we got to the house, the tighter the knot grew in my stomach. I had no idea what I was going to do or how I was going to do it. I motioned for him to park on the street instead of pulling directly into the driveway, to buy us a little time.

"So, have you decided what you're going to tell them?"

"Who?"

"Your folks, who else?"

"Oh. Actually, no. But I'll think of something, don't worry. So, what time are you coming back to pick us up?" I looked at the clock on the dash, and it read one thirty-six.

"How about three-thirty?"

"Calvin!" I exclaimed.

"What? Jaycee, I told you we can't be playin' around. We're down to these last few hours as it is —"

"Just give me until four, okay? That will still give us a good two hours to get out of town before Mr. Rawlins comes back looking for us. I just need a little time to figure all of this out."

"I don't see what's so hard to figure out." He got out of the car to unstrap C.J.'s carseat while I gathered my purse and the diaper bag. "You grown now. Just tell them the truth." I shot him a surprised look. "You know what I mean, Jaycee. Tell them we're gettin' married and I got a job transfer, so we're movin'. Now, that's just a little white lie that ain't too far-fetched."

Calvin and his *little, white lies*. I wondered how far he thought they could carry him. He honestly had faith in his little lies just as sure as my grandmother had faith in the Lord. We were at the front door now, and as I reached for the doorknob, he gave me a quick goodbye peck on the cheek and left. He had disappeared in his car before my mother could even answer the door. I shook my head and fixed a big, fake smile on my face for my parents.

* * * * *

Dinner was good as always, which set the tone for conversation, as I asked Mom what was in this and that. She proudly rambled off the ingredients, while eating and making sure Dad wasn't overfeeding C.J., giving me time to mentally prepare my going-away speech. I prayed a quick prayer and took the plunge.

"Mom, Dad. I have something to tell you." All eyes were on me as I began to speak, choosing my words very carefully. "We're leaving town for a while, to go visit Calvin's mother in California. She's a little under the weather, and we thought it might do her some good to see the baby. Calvin said she might have cancer." *Forgive me, Lord.* Calvin's mother was already dead, and she had died from cancer, but it had been over a year ago. My mother seemed to show real concern as she put her fork down and bowed her head in a silent prayer. I felt like a mustard seed. I wasn't sure how Dad was taking the news because, to my surprise, he had become engrossed with the baby, lifting him in the air and carrying on. I started to caution him of the results he would get, considering he had just fed C.J., but thought twice and sustained.

"So, when are you leaving?" asked Mom.

"Tonight — actually in a couple of hours."

"A couple of hours!" exclaimed Mom. "Jaycee, don't you think it's a little soon after just having the baby to go traveling? You really need your rest."

"I know, Mom, but Calvin needs me for support." I knew Dad couldn't keep quiet for too long after that last statement.

"Jaycee, my heart goes out to Mrs. Jones, in more ways than one, trust me. But when is that boy going to take some responsibility on his own and show *you* some support? Your mother's right. You just had this baby. The last thing you need to do is to go traipsing around the country behind this boy. Now, don't take this the wrong way, but maybe the Lord is trying to tell Calvin something, using his mother's illness."

"Daddy!" I couldn't believe what I was hearing.

"Now, listen to me, girl. I know what I'm saying. And I also know about that little so-called job he has. People have been talking around town. He's up to no good, and I wouldn't put it past him if he's gone and got himself into some trouble and is just fooling you with this story, so you can run off with him and be his shield."

"*His shield*? What do you mean by that, Daddy?" My father shook his head and stood up from the table, holding the baby, and looked at my mother. C.J. had started to get fussy and began crying.

"Woman, please talk some sense into that girl while I go lay this baby down."

I pushed my plate aside, ready for battle. "Momma, Calvin really loves me. He's not as bad as Daddy makes him out to be, really." My mother rolled her eyes in pity.

"Jaycee, no one has ever questioned Calvin's *love* for you. He probably really does love you, honey. And I truly, truly believe that you love him with all your heart. But I don't think either one of you has really, really defined the word or the meaning behind it."

Here we go, I thought. Mom was about to go off on one her tangents, again, lecturing me on the game of life.

"See, baby. Real love is not just based on affection towards one another. It's a whole lot deeper than that. You see, you can be affectionate with each other, hug and kiss and do the nasty all day long." *Oh my God, I thought. Why did she have to go there?* "You can even produce a baby as a result of all that affection. But, honey, that's not love. Love protects you from harm. Love takes care of you and sees to your every need. Love makes sure that there's food on the table and in the cupboards. Love keeps the electricity bill current and the phone turned on. Love compromises — not jeopardizes. If a situation arises, love stands ground and deals with the problem at hand —

not runs or drags other people into the situation who have no business."

I scratched the side of my neck and drank some iced tea. *Wow*, I said to myself. *You would've thought they had my apartment bugged or something.* She was hitting everything on the nail, and I couldn't believe it. I had worked so hard to keep all of the bad stuff from them, or so I thought. But they seemed to know everything, the real truth behind every *little white lie* I had ever told. I kept gulping the tea down, thirsting for ammunition. It was always so hard to come back at Mom after one of her speeches.

"Mom, I know what you're saying," *boy, do I know*, "but it's really not like that. Calvin means well. I know he wouldn't put us in any deliberate harm. And he's not running from anything. We are going to California to see his mom, and then he's taking me to the Bahamas to get married."

My mother busted out laughing, almost in hysterics. I had said the Bahamas instead of Acapulco just in case Mr. Rawlins had been following us and wanted to interrogate my parents later. I marveled at how my lies just seemed to come out naturally after awhile. But then, that's what they say, once you tell one lie, you have to keep going to continue covering your tracks.

"I was wondering when that was coming," she said, as she wiped a tear from her eye. "Your father and I have been expecting that one. Well, I'm going to stop preaching now, because I see that you're already too far gone to listen." She stood up from the table. We had been sitting across from each other, face to face. She walked around to my side of the table and lifted up my chin like she used to do when I was little. Suddenly, the expression on her face became real serious. "Baby, you're just going to have to find things out the hard way, on your own. That boy's really got you under his spell, and God knows I've tried to break it. I pray every night for you and that baby in there…"

She stopped talking, and as she walked away, I could see tears welling up in both eyes. I sat there by myself at the table and stared at all of the food that had been prepared and wondered if this was my last good meal for awhile.

And, as if I hadn't been preached at enough, my father came charging in for Round Two.

"Jaycee, what's gotten into you, girl? Your mother just told me that you were thinking about marrying that boy. Now tell me it's not true," he pleaded.

"It is true, Daddy. And I'm not thinking about it. I've already said yes." He hung his head, shaking it in disbelief.

"Baby girl, think about what you're doing. Think about your son. If you don't marry that boy, you can move back home. Your mother and I will do our best to help you. We … we'll even buy you another car." I looked up at him in utter disbelief. "Well, you need a bigger car anyway, now that you have the baby."

"Daddy, I cannot believe my ears. You're bribing me! How could you do that? Don't you understand that I'm not your little girl anymore? I'm a woman now, a mother. And I'm in love. Why can't you be happy for me?" I started sobbing uncontrollably. I was so disturbed by the bribe with a new car, I didn't know how to react. Fortunately, the doorbell rang, and as I looked up at the grandfather clock, which read three fifty-five, I instantly knew it was Calvin. My parents must have sensed who it was, too, because neither one of them bothered to answer the door. Finally, I got up to answer it myself, and sure enough, it was Calvin. I gently pushed him away from the door and joined him outside. I started walking toward the back of the house where there was a swing, built for me years ago by my father. It hung from a magnolia tree which was not in bloom at the moment. Calvin appeared a little bewildered, but followed my cue.

"What's up? Why are we back here? Ain't you ready to go?" If I didn't know any better, I'd say he seemed a bit worried.

"Yeah. My parents are a little freaked right now, that's all. I just told them about us leaving and going off to get married."

"Oh. They not takin' it too well, hunh?"

"Nope. Not at all. You know, they even bribed me to stay?"

"Sho 'nough?"

"Yeah, said that I could move back home, and that they'd buy me a new car. I can't believe them!"

"A new car?" A hint of a smirk began to spread across Calvin's face, and just as quickly as it appeared, I made it disappear with a look of death.

"Oh, don't even —" I muttered as calmly and quietly as possible. "If you so much as utter a word —"

"What, boo? What are you talkin' about?" he asked, now with a full smile. "I wasn't — I was just —" I stopped him with my hand in his face.

"Just stop it right there. I already know you, Calvin. You keep forgetting that. And I know what you were thinking. You know, I have half a mind to leave you standing right here, and go on back in there and stay."

"Peace." Calvin backed up and put his arm out, as if to give me the go-ahead to cross over to the other side.

"Calvin? Now, you don't mean that. I know you don't." I suddenly found myself pleading with him, almost begging him to discard his last remark.

"Look, I'm not the one doubting my love here. Apparently you don't really love me and you don't know what you want. Talkin' about 'half a mind.' What's that shit about? You half love me and you half want a new car? What, Jaycee? So, maybe you better just stay. 'Cuz I don't have time for some little country-ass girl who don't know what she wants. I need a real woman who's down for me. You know what I'm sayin'? Through thick and through thin, for better or for worse, like the vows say." I started crying and walked over to him, taking his hands.

"Baby, I do love you. Haven't I always been there for you for better or for worse? Have you forgotten everything we've been through in just the last twenty-four hours? Hunh? I was right there when those guys were in our front room with guns. I was even there for you when you told me not to be —" I broke down in tears and just sat there on the grass, on my knees, in despair.

I didn't really know what to do. I was so confused. I loved my parents — and I loved Calvin. I couldn't understand why they were all making me choose. Why couldn't I just love them all the same? Why did I have to pick one over the other? Why were those men really after Calvin? Why did we have to leave? Why couldn't my parents take us all in — me, the baby and Calvin? Like normal parents do when their children get married with a young family? Why, why? All these questions, with no answers, kept swirling through my head. I could even see the question marks flying around, all neon colors against a pitch-black canvas. Calvin bent down on his knees in front of me and took my hands.

"Jay, I love you with all my heart. I do. And I know you down for me. That was just talk. You just scared me there for a minute. I thought you was about to bounce, that's all. But we can do this thing, girl. For real. We didn't come all this way for nothin'. Everything we go through is just gonna make our relationship that much stronger. I know this. But you have to believe that, too, Jaycee.

And you have to believe in me," he searched my eyes for confirmation.

"I do, Calvin," I nodded my head yes. "I believe in you, honest."

"Then let's do this." He stood up and reached his hand out to me, and I joined him as we both started back slowly toward the house.

"So, what are you gonna tell your folks?"

"I don't know. But it doesn't really matter. They're not going to understand or change their feelings about the whole thing."

"It's not going to be a big production, is it?"

"Too late for that. We had a big fight already, just before you came."

"Oh."

We finally made our way to the front porch, and I grabbed hold of Calvin's hand, like my life depended on it, as I turned the doorknob to enter the battlefield for Round Three. My parents were both sitting on the couch, almost at attention. They looked like they were pretending to watch TV, but to no avail.

"Mom, Daddy. I've made my decision. I'm still going to leave with Calvin. We're going to get married, and that's that. I'm all grown up now, and you'll just have to learn to accept that. In time, I'm sure things will get better, and everyone will learn to like each other. Hmm?" I looked at the three of them, one by one, for assured responses. Calvin nodded his head for me and smiled. But my parents just sat there on the couch, rigid and mute, like statues. The room was so quiet, you could have heard a pin drop.

The phone rang, and my father got up to answer it. I could tell it was someone from the church because he referred to him as "Brother" before saying his name. Then my mother suddenly got this "I left something in the oven" expression on her face and rushed off to the kitchen without uttering a word. They both acted like we hadn't even entered their presence. I waited for Daddy to get off the phone, but he never did. He just stood by the window with his back to us, pretending to be in some deep discussion about adding more pews in the sanctuary or what have you. He was in charge of the Building Fund.

Reluctantly, I abandoned Calvin in order to hunt my mother down. He assured me he'd be fine until I returned, but inched a little closer to the front door in case a speedy exit was necessary. I found her in the kitchen, placing an apple pie on a cooling rack. It did appear to have browned a shade darker than her normal liking, but still looked good enough to eat, if you asked me.

"Mom?" I waited for her to answer, but she didn't. So I walked up to her and grabbed her hand, gently forcing her to communicate with me. "Mom, I really need your blessing on this one. You've got to talk to me. Say something — say anything. Just don't block me out, please," I begged her. "I can't stand it."

I was used to Dad ignoring me, but not her, too. The only time my father ever really acknowledged my existence was if it were life-altering. He had always wanted a boy, so he never took up too much time with me, just relinquished all parental rights to my mother, so to speak. Oh, he helped clothe and feed me and did all the expected things of a paternal provider who lives in the same household. But when it came to one-on-one communication, he preferred for my mom to handle all of the answers to, "Can I do this? Can I do that? Why can't I do it? When can I do it?" and so on and so forth. And it was funny how I could always tell when the answer was a sure Yes or an ultimate No, depending on the way my mother answered me.

I remember asking my mother once if I could go to a school dance. The dispute wasn't with me wanting to go.

It was that I wanted to go *with* someone. It was my freshman year at Piermont High, and I was just dying to ask Robert Jackson to the Sadie Hawkins dance. He was the finest boy in ninth grade. But first I had to make sure I could go myself. Or that would've been like trying to "hitch the wagon before you have a horse," according to my grandmother.

* * * * *

"Mom?"

"Yes, baby."

"Can I go to the dance on Friday? You gotta answer me right away 'cause it's a Sadie Hawkins dance which means the girl has to ask the boy, and I want to ask Robert Jackson, and if I don't hurry up and ask him, someone else might get to him first —"

"Excuse me, missy." Mom gave me her infamous "talk to the hand" sign. "Hold your britches. First of all, don't come telling me when I have to give you an answer. That will surely get you a 'NO' real quick. You hear me?"

"Yes, ma'am. I just meant that I don't have much time. He's only the cutest boy in the ninth grade and everybody wants him – I mean – everybody wants to go out with him." Mom started smiling.

"I know what you meant. Remember, I was a teenager once. Let me talk to your father about it and I will get back to you—"

"Oh, Mom."

"What, girl?"

"Now, you know he's going to say no. He doesn't like me liking boys yet. If you tell him, he'll surely say no."

"Well, I can't *not* tell him, Jaycee. He's your father. What do you want me to do, sneak you out of the house and pretend I don't know where you're going?"

"Hey, that's an idea —" I said, smiling.

"Jaycee Washington!" exclaimed my mother. "Why, I don't believe you, wanting to defy your father like that. Young lady, you ought to be ashamed of yourself." She walked away, shaking her head in disbelief. Later, I was told I could go — and was even given permission to ask Robert, but under the condition that we would be fully chaperoned — from start to finish, no drop-offs and pick-ups. I was completely dismayed and forfeited my request in the end. Kyra Wilson ended up being Robert's lucky date.

* * * * *

My mother squeezed my hand back. It was the first sign of response that she had given me.

"Jaycee, I love you with all my heart. And your father loves you, too. You know that. We know what it's like to be young and in love. But we just have a bad feeling about this Calvin. Everything he's saying isn't all up to par. Honey, we've heard too many bad things about him. And we just don't want you or the baby to get hurt by being wrapped up in all of his mess."

I put my head down in defeat, knowing that every word she was saying was right. But I couldn't bring myself to loosen from Calvin's strings. I truly loved him and couldn't imagine my world without him, especially now that we had a son together. C.J. was all ours and no one else's. He was a symbol of our love. Now, how could I deliberately break those ties and leave Calvin? I watched my mother fiddle with the pies and noticed her wedding ring. It reminded me of my ring for an instant. I lost myself in its glow for a second, as if I were looking into a crystal ball, hoping it would miraculously give off some kind of calming spirit to fix everything for me. Then I looked down at my bare hand and longed to have my own ring back. I hated Rawlins for taking it and secretly wished him dead ... or at least violently sick for an indefinite time.

"Jaycee," she said, taking both of my hands into hers, after briskly wiping away an escaped tear from her right eye. "Like I told your father, you're going to do what you want, no matter how much we fight and preach to you to do the opposite. Frankly, I gave up this fight a long time ago on trying to steer you away from that boy. Because I know how strong love can put a grip on you, whether it's good love or bad love, it's still love and once you're in it, it's hard to just take your foot and step right back out of it. It doesn't work like that —"

"Oh, Mom. See, I knew you'd see things my way," I exclaimed and hugged her. "Now if you could just get Dad —"

"Now, hold on a minute," my mother stopped me in mid-sentence. "I don't see any of this your way. Don't get me wrong. I stand strongly beside your father when he says he doesn't approve of Calvin or his lifestyle — I don't either, not in the least. I'm just telling you that I'm through fighting you on this, and baby, I'm just going to let you go and let God work this out. He will see us through this. I believe that with all my heart and soul. You just remember one thing ... that when you finally wake up and smell the coffee and get truly tired of it all, that you know where home is and all you have to do is pick up the phone and tell us you're coming home, and we'll make sure that you're on the next flight out of wherever you're at. You hear me, girl?" She lifted up my chin to look me in the eyes. I had lowered my head, defeated once again by her words of righteousness. They were always good weapons against an opponent. Especially when the opponent was me. We hugged one last time, then we both straightened up to go back into the other room where Calvin and my father awaited. My mother followed me into the guest room where C.J. was still sleeping and helped me get him ready to go.

"Mom, I hear what you're saying. Honestly, I do. But this is something that I have to do, like you said. I have to give this thing with Calvin a chance. After all, he is the father of my child. How can I just let him go like the wind? A son needs his father. And doesn't every home need a man?"

"Jaycee, a home is what you make of it. Black women have been raising children on their own for decades. You wouldn't be the first, nor will you be the last. And besides, you would have me and your father to help. You know that." She stood up from the bed and placed the diaper bag on my left shoulder for me. I looked at that as her gesture of defeat. I had already put C.J. in his carseat and was holding him up with my right hand. Together we walked into the living room.

Calvin was still standing by the door, and my father, now off of the phone, had resumed his position in the window, staring off into nothing, avoiding me altogether. I walked up to him with the baby, hoping C.J. might soften the blow of my departure. On cue, C.J. woke up from his nap and began cooing as if he were talking to Dad on my behalf. It must have worked because Dad turned around to look at him. He bent down and kissed him goodbye on the forehead without once looking up at me. That really hurt and I winced briefly, trying to hold back tears of rejection.

"Goodbye, Daddy," I managed to falter. "I love you." I waited for his response, but none came. Mom came over and walked me to the door with her arms around me. She also kissed C.J. on the forehead.

"You take good care of my babies, you hear me?" she told Calvin, fighting back tears.

"Yes, ma'am." I gave Calvin a quick glance, silently

urging him to keep his words to a minimum, so as not to perpetuate matters at hand. Surprisingly, he picked up on it and opened the front door, proceeding to the car with the baby.

"You remember what I said, Jaycee, about coming home when you get good and ready."

"Okay, Mom. But with all due respect, I hope Calvin proves you and Daddy wrong." As soon as those words came out of my mouth, I yearned to take them back, hoping I wouldn't receive a slap as a rebuttal.

"You know, Jaycee. I can honestly say that I hope he does, too, baby. I hope he does, too."

And that was the last conversation that I had with my mother for almost a year.

Chapter Eight

WE FINALLY REACHED Tulsa, Oklahoma, around eight-thirty. Calvin had promised me that we would reschedule our honeymoon trip to Acapulco just as soon as he worked some things out with the whole Rawlins deal. We had mutually decided that we should divert our plans after reflecting on the little episode at the apartment with his gurus. As big as bullies they were, they were not in the least bit stupid. They were still drug dealers, after all. So we couldn't undermine their intelligence on whether they had picked up on all of the brochures we had lying all over the coffee table. The decision was actually my idea, but I silently mourned the loss of opportunity to an exotic island, knowing in my heart that we would probably never get another chance to go.

The drive completely wiped us out, so we stopped off at a motel for the night, with plans of heading on to Tulsa in the morning. Calvin had mentioned having a cousin there who could put us up for a couple of weeks until we were ready to go to California. I had asked Calvin about the so-called layover, but he had carried on about making some extra "ends" he called it, just to be on the safe side.

After putting C.J. down, I went and took a shower, and still reflecting on the money thing, I confronted Calvin in midstream of my thoughts.

"But, Calvin, what did you do with all of that cash I saw back at the apartment? We should have plenty of money to get to California and Timbuktu — and back."

"Baby, that wasn't as much money as you thought it was. And, like you guessed, some of it wasn't mine. I had to make a couple of stops and pay some people back while you were saying your farewells to your folks. Not to mention these — tadow — plane tickets to Acapulco!"

"Calvin Lee Jones!" I exclaimed in delight. "How could you trick me like that? You know how bad I wanted to go on that trip and you knew all along!" All he could do was laugh at me. I eventually joined in, happy for the surprise. It was finally a change in the script that I didn't mind. Then, as an afterthought, "Hey, what are we going to do about C.J.? I can't just call up my parents now and ask them to babysit."

"Were you really goin' to in the first place?" He had a point there that I couldn't argue with. I guess I hadn't really thought about it until now. Before we had needed to move so suddenly, I just naturally assumed my parents would help us out in the long run. I hadn't made many girlfriends since high school, so my parents were the only option. "I could probably get my cousin, Lisa, to watch him while we're gone since we'll be stayin' there anyway. She don't work and already has four kids. What's one more gonna hurt?"

"Easy for you to say. That's the last thing she needs is *one more*, especially a newborn baby. Don't you think we're imposing on her enough by having to stay there at all. Now you want her to babysit so we can run off to some exotic island without a care in the world?"

"Look, do you want to go or not?"

"Why can't we take him with us?"

" 'Cause then it wouldn't really be too much of a honeymoon, now would it? By the time you get done feedin' and changin' him every two or three hours, you'll be too tired to take care of me, then that would be defeatin' the purpose of the whole trip." I immediately went on the defense with that little remark.

"So, our honeymoon is about me taking care of you? I thought we're supposed to take care of each other, Calvin. I take damn good care of you right here in America. I don't need to go all the way across the world to another country to do that."

"Fine. Then we won't go." He got up, threw the tickets away and stormed into the bathroom, slamming the door behind him. I had not meant for that to happen at all. I instantly felt bad and tried to make amends through the door, but to no avail.

"Calvin, baby, I'm sorry. I didn't mean it like that. I still want to go." He didn't say anything, but I heard the shower come on, washing away my voice, so I backed off in defeat. I went on to bed and waited for him to come out. I heard him turn the water off, but it seemed like forever before he came out. When he finally did, he looked worse than he did before he went in. His forehead was dripping with either sweat or water, I couldn't tell because he was still fully dressed. And his eyes were kind of glazed over, like when you first wake up in the morning. *He must be exhausted from all of that driving,* I thought. I assumed the sweat was probably from the steam of the hot water running so long. So I dismissed his poor appearance and I sat up in bed.

"I thought you were taking a shower," I said.

"I'll take one in the morning before we go," he said calmly.

"Then why did you have the water running for so long if you weren't in it?"

"What are you, water patrol, now? Damn, what's up with the third degree?" he asked, not so calm now.

"Well, Calvin. It just doesn't make sense. I could see you trying to wash me out and not wanting to talk to me. But you must have known that I wasn't going to keep talking through the door like that. I know how to take a hint."

"You sure about that?" he asked sarcastically. "You've been known to keep drivin' shit into the ground, like you're doin' right about now." I glared at him.

"Fine. Just drop the whole thing. I just think it's a little strange you not going ahead and actually getting in the shower, no matter what the reason. It's not like you don't need to take one after such a long trip. Forgive me for wondering why you're acting so weird all of a sudden. And why do you keep sniffing? You trying to catch a cold or something?"

"Girl, if you ask me one more question, I swear —" After having his back to me, he had abruptly turned over and put his finger in my face. I couldn't believe his actions. In fact, out of shock, I guess, I made the situation even worse by going on my own little trip. I slapped his hand down, out of my face. Then he grabbed my arm and it was on. I got out of the bed and stood up.

"What the hell is wrong with you? Don't you ever put your hand in my face or touch me like that again or I'm out of here. Do you hear me? I demand more respect than that. I am not your wife yet, okay. And you keep this shit up, I might not be at all."

"Look, you hit me first." He sounded like a six-year-old or something. "I didn't touch you until after you hit me, Jaycee. So don't start acting like I'm some wife-beater or somethin'. You're the one trippin' —"

"I'm the one trippin'? Why are you putting your hand in my face like that, like I'm a child or something?"

"*Why are you putting your hand in my face like that?*" he mocked me. "You know, Jaycee, maybe this was a mistake bringing you here with me. I'm getting tired of your little proper, self-righteous ass."

"What?!" Now my shock had gone to pure dismay. "I can't believe what I'm hearing, Calvin. Now you want to dump me after I choose you over my parents? Well, isn't that convenient?"

"How is it convenient for me?" he asked innocently.

"Because now you think you have me where you want me. You know that I can't just run back to my parents. So you're taking advantage of that and using it against me by acting like you want to break up. You know, I'm not going to go back home so fast, so they can tell me, 'I told you so.'"

"Oh, so it's all about you, hunh?" he cleverly turned the tables on me, using my own words for backfire. "This — this whole thing is about Jaycee — not Jaycee and Calvin. I'm the one bein' used. I'm just a little pawn in this tug of war you're havin' with your parents. Tell me somethin', Jaycee, is our whole relationship just based on rebellion against your folks? And C.J., is he just another pawn to get back at them —"

"Now stop it right there. You leave our son out of this. How dare you question me about my love for him or you. You've got some nerve. You can't even begin to understand how much the two of you mean to me. I just gave up two of the most important people in my entire life for the two of you. Now, if that's not love, then I don't know what is. Do you know how much of a sacrifice that was? Well, of course not," I answered myself. "Look who I'm talking to." And with that, I stomped off to the bathroom.

When I returned, C.J. was still sleeping, and Calvin was nowhere to be found. I invited the quiet and decided to take a nap until C.J.'s next feeding. Like clockwork, he woke up around one o'clock in the morning, and there was still no Calvin. He had been gone for over two hours now. I tried not to worry as I went into the bathroom to warm up a bottle under the faucet. I comforted myself in watching C.J. marvel at his new surroundings. The color scheme had been poorly chosen with black and white checkers bordering a pale blue wall. I guess they had wanted to match the checkered tile on the floor. To me, it was an obvious fashion glitch. But to C.J. it was a work of art, something new and exciting to his little eyes. I had read somewhere in a baby magazine that babies tended to notice basic colors, like the primary red, blue and yellow. But that more often than not, they really focused on things that were in black and white. I guess the whole contrast thing is what gets their attention.

As I threw the paper towel in the trash that I had used to dry off the bottle, something long and shiny caught my eye. Curious, I pulled it out, and it appeared to be some type of antenna, like from a TV or radio. One end was a little black like maybe it had been burnt or something. The TV or radio must have blown a fuse and messed it up. I shrugged my shoulders, put it back in the trash and focused my attention back on the baby. I washed my hands and returned to the bedroom to feed C.J. I put him back to sleep and tried to go back to sleep myself, but to no avail.

I thought about my parents and contemplated calling them, but knew that it was too late in the night. The phone ringing at such an hour would surely startle them. I didn't even know what I wanted to say. I just wanted to hear their voices. I suddenly felt so alone in the world. Calvin's frequent departures after a fight had begun to take its toll on my self-esteem, especially when it was late at night. I couldn't help but think that he was off somewhere finding comfort in another woman's arms. I looked around to see if the keys were still on the table by the window, and they were. So he had fled on foot again, off into the night to God knows where.

Before the baby came, he would take off in my car. I

never even knew my keys were missing until it was too late. I would borrow the neighbor's car and eventually find him at some friend's house and beg him to come home. But now that C.J. was here, I hardly had time for cat and mouse games with his daddy. Besides, I hadn't a clue of where to begin to look for him. I was in unfamiliar territory, and the last thing I needed to do was go roaming around a strange town with a newborn baby in the middle of the night. I went back to bed and let the low hum of the heater put me back to sleep.

Eventually, Calvin came back. I didn't even bother to get up and drill him or check the time. Instead of arguing, I decided to sleep. I heard him use the restroom and take off his clothes; then he finally came to bed. I had learned to sleep lightly while still absorbing my surroundings, partly due to new motherhood, but mostly due to being a part of Calvin's world. It's strange how precious things such as sleep and peace of mind a woman can give up for the love of a man.

Chapter Nine

I WOKE UP, exhausted, at a quarter to six. A strip of sun glistened through the curtains over the heater. I sat up in bed and looked over at the lump of covers lying beside me, slightly moving up and down. A question crossed my mind as to whether or not I was prepared to live with this lump for the rest of my life. Then I glanced over at the little lump lying in the crib across from us, and that was enough to answer yes.

There was a little green Bible on the nightstand that I had noticed when we checked in. It had been pushed aside by a couple of pop cans, an ashtray which held my watch and earrings, and other various last-minute items which respectively consume such a piece of furniture. I was moved to retrieve it and tiptoe to the bathroom.

I hadn't opened a Bible in a long time, actually since I had met Calvin. My daily devotions, from when I lived at home, had turned into weekly devotions after I left, until there were no devotions once Calvin and I had decided to move in together. It seemed I only spent time with God when things would get kind of rough, and I needed Him to know that I was acknowledging my faults, but didn't want Him to give up on me — or Calvin. You see, it didn't matter how far I strayed from Him, I was taught that I could always call on Him and He would always hear me — whether He answered me right away or not.

I thumbed through the pages seeking some kind of direction, until my fingers rested on the book of Romans. There, I found a passage in the eighth chapter where it speaks of the flesh versus the spirit and the tug of war that we as humans face with having naturally carnal minds. I really felt that this chapter was talking to me. It characterized what I was going through every day with Calvin; earnestly wanting to live right, but also wanting to love and please Calvin at the same time. It would take me long time to figure out that the two did not — and cannot mix.

Tears welled up in my eyes, the more I read, knowing in my heart what was the right thing to do, but again fighting it and choosing to keep riding the fence. I read the chapter over and over, trying to pull something out of it to hold on to and keep me through all of the turmoil that I was enduring with Calvin and carry me through what was yet to come. Finally, the twenty-eighth verse engaged me and promised me that everything would be okay in due time ... "And we know that all things work together for good to them that love God, to them who are the called according to *his* purpose." I adopted that verse and chanted it over and over until I had it memorized. It became my rod and my staff. I was overwhelmed with a sudden peace that I hadn't felt since I had lived at home with my parents.

For the first time in a long time, I heard knocking outside the bathroom door and didn't jump. It was only housekeeping. We had forgotten to hang the *Do Not Disturb* sign on the knob. I politely asked them to come back in Spanish, and they both giggled in surprise, but responded and went on their way. As I closed the door, I could hear them rambling in their native tongue. I didn't understand all of the words, but gathered that they were wondering how I knew their language. I giggled in spite of myself, always enjoying the opportunity to show off and reveal my hidden talents when the occasion arose.

"What's so funny so early in the morning?" asked Calvin, a little grumpily. "And who in the hell was that knockin' at the door?"

"It was housekeeping. You forgot to put the sign on the door when you came in last night." I wanted to say *this morning*, but decided against it. What I had said must have been just enough because he didn't say anything back, or at least not anything pertaining to the subject.

"What time is it anyway?" he asked, rolling over to look at the clock on the nightstand. "It's only seven o'clock! What were they doin' here so damn early anyway?" *My, aren't we the cranky one this morning, I thought to myself. Maybe if we had come in at a decent time — or better yet, kept our butt here to begin with and gone on to bed …*

"Honey, they're just doing their job. We're the ones that didn't do ours by not hanging the sign up." *Oh, now wasn't that a nice way of putting it, but still telling him off without him realizing it, I told myself. Gosh, I wondered, how different the world would be if everyone got up and read their Bible first thing in the morning before engaging in conversation …"*

"Whatever," Calvin mumbled. "What happened to tact?"

"Tact?" I asked, laughing. "Calvin, it's their *job*. Housekeeping aren't taught tact. They're trained to get as many rooms cleaned as they can by a certain time in the morning. The only tact that's used is not barging in *after* they've seen the sign on the door."

"Right," even Calvin cracked a smile at that comment. "Well, since we're up and awake now, what do you want for breakfast? You want me to go get some donuts or

Mickey D's or somethin'?" Just like that, he seemed to snap back to his old self. He seemed to do that more often; one minute he'd be tripping and going off about something, then the next minute he'd be sailing smoothly with little or no waves. It was very odd.

"Mmm, bagels with strawberry cream cheese sound really good. Do they have a café here?"

"No, Dorothy, we ain't in Kansas no mo'," Calvin joked. "This is the hood, baby. All we have here are donuts. That's as close as you're gonna get to your fancy little bagels."

"What's wrong with bagels?" I asked in defense. "Calvin, just because a person likes a particular kind of food doesn't make them snooty like you're implying."

"Snoo-ty?" he raved in a humorous, English accent, conveying a hidden talent of his own. He was very good at impersonating people with different accents. He would have made a great comedian. I hadn't said it quite like that, but I had put my foot in my mouth with that comment, and he ran with it.

We both laughed as I playfully snapped him with one of the baby's blankets and missed. He grabbed the end of it with his left hand and pulled me toward him as we fell onto the bed. It almost felt like we were back at home in the apartment, happy and peaceful, before all of the chaos.

"Calvin?"

"What," he asked as he began to nibble on my left ear. So many things were running through my mind. I wanted to ask him if we had done the right thing by running away? If he thought we were going to be okay from now on? Did we lose the bad guys? Was the running over? And on and on, as if he were my magic genie with all of the answers. And deep down in my heart, I knew he wasn't.

"Nothing," I said, closing my eyes.

I dismissed my doubts and let the moment sweep me away as he began to kiss me slowly and with such tenderness, meanwhile untying the drawstring to my sweatpants and fondling my inner thighs. I moaned in delight. He stopped kissing me to pull my shirt off and occupy his mouth with one of my breasts, softly caressing my nipple with his tongue. And when he had succeeded, he ventured to the other breast and did the same. I soon reached my peak between that and his crafty handwork down below, and was fully aroused, ready for the next stage. He finished undressing me along with himself until we were both completely naked and ready for engagement. His lips found my lips again as our bodies slowly meshed until we were one, rocking and swaying without the aid of any music. For our bodies seemed to have a rhythm of their own.

"You still want donuts?" he whispered in my ear.

"Un-unh," I managed to respond.

Chapter Ten

WE SHOWERED TOGETHER and almost had seconds until the sound of our son stopped us. I quickly got out to dress and prepare another bottle. Calvin packed as I fed C.J. and we were checked out and on our way to Lisa's house just before noon.

We turned into an apartment complex on Third Street, and I must say I was very surprised. Calvin had told me that Lisa lived in a housing project under Section 8, so I had prepared myself for the worst, reminding myself of housing projects back home. But when we pulled up, there was a security gate at the entrance where Calvin had to punch a code in to open it, and there were flower beds — and even a water fountain built into a median beyond the gate. It was very impressive and nothing like any housing project I'd ever seen back home. I made a quick mental note to write home and tell my mother about it. She had a friend who worked for a housing development company for low-income families. Her friend was always complaining about current conditions and looking for new and creative ways to spice up the facilities. This was definitely an idea for sorts.

We walked up to her building to find her on the third floor. I wasn't too thrilled about climbing the stairs and wondered why they hadn't installed elevators. It would have been a nice touch along with the view of the water fountain entrance. I've always hated half-steppers ... you know, those individuals who have a great idea, but then they mess it up by not thinking things all the way through. For instance, the contractors who built this complex with their grand entrance, just to lead you into an uninviting stairwell ... or the woman wearing the cold, Jacqueline Kennedy black-and-white dress, with the hat and earrings to match, and you know she's got it together until you look down at her shoes ... need I go on? I'm sure you get my point.

So, we finally arrived at the top of the palace and instantly heard muffled cries from various toddler voices, presumably all dwelling in Apartment 315, our destination. *Oh, yea*, I thought, *let the fun begin* ... Calvin had promised me that we would only be staying with her for a maximum of two weeks after we were back from our honeymoon. I had agreed to it and even submitted to allowing Lisa to watch C.J. for us while we were gone. It was now Monday, February thirteenth, and I had less than twenty-four hours to bond with my nanny before the big day. Damn, so much had happened since Saturday when we were all happy in our own apartment, standing in our own kitchen, and picking dates on our wall calendar. I looked around at our new surroundings and suddenly felt a wave of homesickness.

"Excuse me, where's the bathroom?" I asked. Lisa pointed and it was all I could do to sprint to the bathroom to keep from blessing her carpet. I practically had to toss C.J. to Calvin on the way. It was not the first impression I had wanted to give, but an unforgettable one nonetheless.

"You sure she still ain't got one up in her?" I heard her ask Calvin, jokingly. I turned to the door as if I was looking right at her and rolled my eyes. This was not getting off to a good start. I flushed the toilet, splashed my face with cold water and returned to the living room for a retake.

"You okay, love?" she asked, grabbing my hand and swinging it like we were little girls on a playground. In an instant, she reminded me of Calvin. Her smart remark had bothered me, but on the other hand, she had seemed genuinely concerned about me, and her warm smile had melted me down a notch.

"Yeah," I returned her smile. "I'm fine, must be leftover carsickness from the drive down here. Sorry for messing up your bathroom. I cleaned it up, but I'll scrub your toilet for you later if you want," I gestured.

"Girl, please. Don't pay that bathroom no mind. The maid will get it." I looked at her funny and we both started laughing uncontrollably.

She was quite the comic, but her nonchalance lightened the mood and put my mind at ease, for a change. Lisa really did have a nice smile, quite similar to Calvin's — big and carefree — and I wondered if it was hereditary. They were first cousins, after all. The only difference was that her smile was accented with a hint of diamond in one tooth on the top row. She was a medium brown, like me and Calvin ... the color of walnut, yet her skin seemed to radiate with cheer and great vigor. I reckoned she couldn't help but be alive with four little ones scrambling all over the house. I had to give it to her, raising a family alone without any help from a man. Calvin had told me that she had been married once or twice, but it never worked out. He had known both husbands and claimed that both divorces were Lisa's fault because she had too much mouth and wanted to be too independent. I begged to differ with him, but hoped it never happened to me, getting left behind with four children to raise on my own. I shuddered at the thought.

"You cold, love?" she asked, going to check the thermostat. It was February after all, but her heat was working just fine.

"No, don't adjust the heat on my account. I'm fine, just got the chills for a sec."

"It's not a problem," she assured me with that friendly smile. "We want our guests to be comfortable." She walked back over to join us on the couch, followed by her miniature entourage. She reached to take C.J. from Calvin, and her youngest one protested by falling out on the floor and throwing a little hissy fit. We all laughed at her impulsive performance. Lisa moved C.J. to one arm and motioned for her jealous two-year old to join her on her lap with her free arm.

"Now, see what y'all have to look forward to when the next one comes?" she warned us, smiling.

"Right," Calvin chuckled, nodding his head.

"No, left, " I protested, shaking my head. "He's not even two months old yet. Please don't jinx me — anytime soon. That's bad luck to give two people getting ready to go on a honeymoon," I said. We all laughed again, and Lisa winked at me. I felt like I had known her my whole life. She seemed to make everything feel all right, and I wondered if she was secretly going to be our guardian angel.

"Bad luck?" Calvin reproached. "I thought you're supposed to make babies on your honeymoon…"

"That's only if you don't already have some," Lisa answered for me.

"Right," I said, returning her wink.

"Pssh," sighed Calvin," whatever."

Chapter Eleven

"C'MON, GIRL. We're gonna miss the plane if we don't get a move on." I had been trying to say goodbye to C.J. for over fifteen minutes now, but couldn't bring myself to hand him over to Lisa who was patiently waiting. I briskly wiped a tear, trying not to completely lose my bearings and call the whole thing off.

"You be good for your cousin, Boo. You hear me? Mommy loves you," I murmured as he gurgled and cooed, as if in mutual response. I kissed him on the forehead a few more times and rapidly went over his feeding times and sleeping habits again with Lisa as she gently took him from my arms.

"Okay, Jay," she said, nodding her head and shooing me away. "I got it. Don't worry. You go on now. He's in good hands. He's with kinfolk. Okay?" she smiled and looked me in the eye.

"Okay," I said, sighing. Calvin grabbed my hand and practically dragged me out of the apartment.

* * * * *

We boarded the plane and Calvin gave me a piece of bubble gum.

"Here, chew this. It'll help your ears." I frowned in bewilderment, but took the gum anyway.

"Hunh? What's going to happen to my ears?" He just

laughed and shook his head, knowing that this was my first flight.

"Jay, your ears pop when you're flyin' in an airplane. It's because of the change in the altitude." For the first time, I felt like the foolish one instead of the other way around.

"Oh," is all I could say.

I believe I spent more time in the bathroom than I did sitting beside Calvin on the plane. I don't know if it was nervousness from being on a plane for the first time, or just pure excitement from the whole trip, but whatever it was, Calvin seemed to be very amused. He kept laughing at me each time I got up to go, and I was very relieved once the stewardess prohibited me from getting up the last time and informed us to buckle up for the landing.

It was kind of a bumpy landing, and I clung to Calvin's side as close as the seats would allow and squeezed his hand as tight as I could.

"Acapulco, here we be," said Calvin, smiling at me. I tried to return his smile, but ended up groping for the emergency airsick bag for one last hurl. I prayed for my nausea not to linger throughout the whole trip.

We stepped off the plane, and I thought I had entered a tropical paradise. That's exactly what it was, with blue water and sandy beaches and tall palm trees. My nausea left just as soon as it had begun. and I looked up toward the heavens and mouthed a "Thank you," smiling.

"You're welcome, baby," replied Calvin, kissing me on the cheek. I started to correct him, but quickly shunned myself and let him bask in his glory.

We checked into our room, and I made a beeline to the bathroom to brush my teeth and take a quick shower. When I returned to the bedroom, there were two pink gift boxes lying on the bed. One was big and one was small. I squealed and grabbed the small one first, already knowing it could only be one thing. I unwrapped it and squealed again. It was another wedding ring, exactly like my first one.

"Now, this one's for me," he said, opening the other box himself to reveal a pink, lace teddy. I dropped my towel and put it on. That lasted all of five minutes before we were passionately engaged in our first round of lovemaking.

The sun set and rose again before we ever left the room.

We woke up the next morning, and I showered and changed into a white sundress I had borrowed from Lisa, and Calvin wore a white t-shirt with white dockers. We went to the front desk and got directions to the Justice of the Peace, which was just two doors down from the hotel, and were wed in holy matrimony within a matter of minutes. We were just one day late from our original date, but I wasn't even mad that we had missed it, just glad that we had finally done it at all. We walked back to our room; Calvin called for a bottle of champagne and again we resumed our lovemaking from the night before.

This time it seemed to be more sensual than ever, and I wondered if the "paper" really did make a difference. We kissed each other from head to toe for hours it seemed before we even made love. It was the best foreplay I had ever experienced with Calvin, and we both climaxed a couple of times without penetration, taking turns being the pleaser as if we were trying to outdo each other. And each time I reached my peak, I thought it was surely the last time, but then Calvin would find that spot just behind my earlobe that I liked so much, and I would regain my energy for another course.

And so it went for our entire trip, and all I can remember of Acapulco is those four walls of the bedroom and a brief picture of the waves hitting the sand at night from the terrace, in between one of our pillow sessions.

Chapter Twelve

WE ARRIVED BACK in Oklahoma after four days and three nights of around-the-clock lovemaking, and I thought I was going to die from having overindulged myself.

Our flight landed around ten o'clock on a Friday night, and we entered the apartment to find Lisa and the kids sound asleep, including C.J. I quickly took the hint and collapsed on the first available vacancy, which was the couch in the living room. It was actually a sectional with a hideaway bed, but I didn't give Calvin a chance to let it out. I just grabbed a nearby blanket and made myself comfortable at one end, still in my clothes. He didn't seem to put up much of a fuss, but followed my cue and retired at the other end of the couch. And we both fell asleep, our bodies spent from the honeymoon I would never forget.

* * * * *

I woke up to the smell of bacon and eggs frying in the kitchen. Lisa was standing against the stove, holding C.J. She looked like a pro, standing sideways, with C.J. positioned in the crook of her arms on her left side which was away from the stove, and turning the bacon with her right hand. I guess it was only natural, considering she had four children of her own. But being the new, overprotective mother that I was, I walked over and politely took him from her, fearing some stray grease might pop on him.

"There's my little man. Good Morning, Boo! How are you? Hunh? How's Mommy's little boy?" He felt like he had gained a pound or two, or else I was still a little fatigued from the trip. He was a little over a month old now and had started filling out more in his face and under his neck where there was once a lot of wrinkles. I grabbed his bottle from the counter and pulled a chair out from the kitchen table to finish feeding him.. I finally noticed that Calvin was nowhere to be found.

"Where's Calvin?" I asked, looking around.

"Oh, I sent him to the store about an hour ago," she said, looking at the clock on the wall.

"An hour ago?" I asked, frowning.

"Yeah, to get some milk for the kids. And I needed some to make the pancakes. But he should have been back by now. He must have run into somebody he knew — which I wouldn't be surprised. It is his hometown after all." I looked up at her in surprise.

"What?"

"What?" she asked back, turning around to look at me.

"You said it's his hometown. I thought he was from California?"

"California — his dad lives in L.A. now," she replied, turning back around to face the stove, but it seemed more like she was avoiding looking me in the eye.

"L.A.? I thought it was Hollywood — and what do you mean now, like he used to live somewhere else? Calvin was born there."

"Hollywood, L.A., whatever. It's all the same to me, miles away from here, right?" She remained in position with her back to me and didn't fully answer me.

"Right. But about Calvin. He's not from here, right. He's from Hollywood, California, born and raised, right?"

"Is that what he told you?" she asked me, now looking me in the eye.

"Yes. That's what he said."

"Then if that's what he said, then that's what it is. Don't mind me none. Always believe your man, Jaycee — unless, of course, it's an ex of mine — then you'd better watch out and go get a second opinion." She started laughing and I joined her. She always knew what to say at the right time to ease the moment. But in the back of my mind, I stored the incident for a future conversation with Mr. Jones … in the very near future.

C.J. had fallen asleep in my arms, so I laid him down on the couch and started helping Lisa fix plates for the kids. Once they were settled, I went back into the living room to sit beside C.J. She followed behind me with a plate.

"Oh, you didn't have to do that. I'm really not all that hungry," I said.

"Girl, please. You need to eat something to regain your strength after that trip. I know y'all didn't come up for air, much less food the whole time you was there." She made me smile, and I turned my head in embarrassment.

"Remember, I've been married a time or two myself, and I still know what it's like — with or without a man in the house — trust!" She nudged me with her elbow and we both started laughing like old friends.

I admired Lisa for being so upbeat about life. I couldn't imagine the things she went through being a single mother and still managing to keep her head above water and run a household all by herself. And she didn't even have to work. With all the money she told me that she received from alimony and child support, you'd have thought she had it made. But she continued to work and stay in a three-bedroom apartment versus a house because she said the expenses were lower, and she was still working on cleaning up some of her bad credit she accrued during her marriages.

"But I thought that this was low-income housing? You still qualified with all of your child support and stuff?" I asked. I was getting a little personal, but knew it was all right. Lisa kind of gave you that impression, that you could talk to her about anything in the world. She started laughing before she answered me.

"Well, I did qualify — before the child support and alimony started rollin' in. I just didn't tell them about it. 'Cause if I would've done that, I'da been kicked out and we'd be livin' over there all scrunched up in a two-bedroom off of 10th and Quinlan where all of the crackheads roam. And I know I'm schemin', but baby, in this world, you gotta do what you gotta do to survive. I have four girls to raise — two, four, nine and ten, and I'm not tryin' to lose them to any bullshit like drugs or prostitution. So, whatever I have to do to send them to the best schools and see that they have the best of everything, then that's what I'm gonna do until I can find a better way." I nodded my head in agreement. "Shit, there's all kind of people gettin' over on the system. But it's not our fault. At first, I was real honest and up front about everything, you know, but it seems like the ones who try to do right are the ones that end up gettin' the short end of the stick. I watched this one heifer move in and out of four different complexes, and each time she was put out for bein' kicked in —"

"Kicked in?" I asked, puzzled.

"Yeah, you know, by the cops. They kicked her door down 'cause she was reported for runnin' a drug house. So, the landlord evicted her and she just literally went from place to place with her little Section 8 voucher and was able to get right in because she was on welfare, didn't work and her kids had medical cards. And here I was, reportin' everything to my caseworker about my job and income, and gettin' the boot for havin' too much income. It's almost like they don't want you to get ahead, like the more down and out you are, the quicker they'll help you, but once they see you tryin' to get up on your feet but still just needin' a little help to get there, they drop you and start takin' away everything until you damn near right back at the bottom." I shook my head in pity at her story, knowing it was the truth. I had heard my parents talk about it too many times with their friends.

There was a tap at the door and it was Calvin, carrying three bags of groceries and two more were sitting at his feet.

"What's all this?" Lisa asked, catching one from falling out of his arms. "All I asked for was some milk, baby boy."

"I know. I just thought I'd help out a little bit since you're puttin' us up and all for a minute."

"For a minute? This looks like you're stayin' for a year!"

"Well, I saw some snacks I wanted to get for the kids."

"For the kids or for *you*?" I asked accusingly.

"Hey," he smiled at me and started to kiss me, but I turned my head and his lips brushed my cheek. He was a little taken aback by my actions, but didn't have the slightest clue of the reason why I was acting like that, and Lisa pretended that she didn't either. I rolled my eyes at him and started toward the kitchen to help Lisa put up the groceries. Calvin shrugged the whole thing off and went into the living room to pick up C.J. who had awakened and started squirming.

"Don't be so hard on the boy just yet," she whispered advice. "Let him explain himself first."

"What does he have to explain if he's telling me the

truth? And why won't you just tell me if he won't? " I asked, pleadingly.

"Because I don't get in people's business like that, Jaycee. Un-unh," she said, shaking her head. "I been burnt too many times before, doing that. And what difference does it really make now anyway? You already married him and y'all just got back from your honeymoon. Don't ruin it over a little nonsense. He was probably just tryin' to impress you at the time …"

"What y'all in here whisperin' about?" Calvin asked, walking up to us with C.J.

"Just girl talk, cousin. Just girl talk," Lisa said, winking at me. I smiled at him and took Lisa's advice for the moment. I guess she was right. But I still wanted to know why he had felt the need to lie to me about being from California. I started to wonder what else he had lied about.

* * * * *

After breakfast, Lisa took the girls to school and daycare and headed off to work. We were finally alone and C.J. was asleep, so I took the opportunity to confront Calvin.

"Calvin?"

"Hunh?" he responded, flipping channels on the television.

"I was talking to Lisa this morning, and she made a comment about this being your hometown. What did she mean by that? I thought you told me that you were from California?"

"I said I was *born* in California and my father lives out there now. That's why we're going out there so I can find a decent job."

"But that's not what you said. You said you were from there, too. That was one of our first conversations, remember? We talked about all the famous people you knew and the actors you went to high school with ... what was all that?" He sighed and put the remote down.

"Okay, so I stretched the truth a little bit. Man, what's up with Lisa gettin' all in my mix like that?"

"No, don't blame Lisa. She's not the one who lied. And she didn't rat you out. I figured it out on my own. In fact, she even sided with you and tried to make excuses for you."

"And what was y'all talkin' about me for in the first place?"

"Because you're the one who was late coming back from the store and she said you had probably bumped into one of your old running buddies or something. And since we're on the subject of the store, what was up with all of that food? I mean, I know she's family and all, but we're only supposed to be here for a few more days. What's with all of the food? And does she know about the money?"

"Damn, what is this, Twenty Questions or Jeopardy or somethin'? If I answer right, do I win a million dollars or at least get to pick what's behind Door Number Two? First of all, I shouldn't have to explain myself about buyin' anything for kinfolk ... food, clothes or whatever the hell I feel like gettin' them at the moment. Okay? And no, Lisa don't know about the money. Even if she did, she wouldn't take any of it from me anyway. She's proud like that. That's why I bought the groceries instead of just handin' her a wad of bills. She can't make me take the food back as easy as she can give me the money back. And with four kids, it's not like she can't use it." He was right about that. I suddenly felt guilty for antagonizing him, then felt foolish for feeling guilty because, once again, Calvin had managed to turn things around, and the very thing that we had started our conversation about did not get addressed.

"Calvin," I said, trying to take a more gentle approach. "Why did you tell me that you were from California if you weren't? You know you didn't have to make all of that up to get my attention."

"But it did help," he returned, and I couldn't disagree with him. It had helped a whole lot, even to the point that I dismissed his means of transportation. I mean, really ... how many girls do you know that would give a brother the time of day on two wheels? Now, maybe a Harley, but not a regular old bicycle for sure. I'm still trying to figure that one out myself. So, that leaves nothing else but the fact that he was fine and was from California, a dream place that I'd never been to.

"Well, it didn't hurt at the time, but now look. You've betrayed my trust and now I can't even depend on your word. I can't tell a lie from the truth ..."

"What are you trippin' about?" he demanded. "So, I go and tell one little white lie and now all of a sudden you can't trust me? So what, you wanna run out and go get a divorce or somethin'?" His question took me by surprise and I didn't know how to react. Normally, I was used to a quick comeback after one of his smart remarks, but not this time. I waited a while before I responded, carefully choosing my words, for fear of making things worse. The last thing I had wanted to do was talk about a divorce while we were virtually still on our honeymoon.

"Calvin, I didn't mean it like that, like I could never trust you ever again." *Well, actually, I had meant it like that, but I couldn't tell him that.* "I just meant that ... if you could lie that easily about something so minute like where you're from, when you didn't even have to, then how do I know when you're telling me the truth when it's something major that I need to know? My parents always told me that if you lie about the little things, you'll lie about the big things ..." And whatever possessed me to say that, I don't know, but the last thing he wanted to hear was about something my parents had said, as if the hole I was digging wasn't big enough.

"So, if you listen to everything your parents tell you, then why did you run off with me, hunh? Why did you marry me?"

"Because I love you."

"Hmph!" he grumbled. "I sho can't tell. If you loved me so much, you would trust me." The famous lines from a renowned smooth-talker. "And I can't be with a woman who doesn't trust me. Just because I told one little story when we first met doesn't mean that everything I say isn't the truth, Jaycee."

Well, how do I know? is what I wanted to say, but I just kept silent and let him win the argument in order to keep the peace. I had only been away from home for only five days and married less than that. I was not about to give up so quickly and go home to hearing a never-ending ballad of "I told you so." No, thank you.

"Okay. You're right," I said. "And so is Lisa. She told me to always believe my man over anybody else."

"Wise words," said Calvin, and he even smiled. And just like that, I had learned how to "bow down" as Lisa put it and soften my husband whenever it was necessary, even if it meant lowering my standards a peg or two in the process. I was desperate to hang onto Calvin, if it killed me, so no matter how bad the advice was, I listened to Lisa and took mental notes, figuring her as a pro after having married twice ... never once questioning why she hadn't taken her own advice and stayed married.

Chapter Thirteen

THREE MONTHS HAD come and gone, and I was itching to confront Calvin and ask him why we hadn't left for California yet, but I feared another outburst from him and a threat of divorce, so I kept my mouth shut and indulged myself in becoming Lisa's little housemaid. I cooked dinner for her so she wouldn't have to come home and start it as soon as she got off work, and I even walked her two older daughters to their bus stop every morning while she left for work with her younger ones. Calvin always slept in and pretended to keep an eye on C.J., but by then I had him on a regular schedule of sleeping through the night, so he often stayed asleep until I was back from dropping the girls off.

One morning, I came back from walking with the girls and overheard Calvin and Lisa in a very intense conversation about money. They were in one of the back bedrooms, so they hadn't heard me come in.

"… Lisa, why are you trippin'? I told you I would take care of you and the girls, didn't I?"

"Well, yeah, but that was before you ran off and got yourself hitched with little Miss Pollyanna. And now you have a baby and — as cute as he is, that wasn't part of our plan, you know "

Plan? I said to myself. What plan? ... And who was she, calling me Pollyanna? I asked myself, a little perturbed. *I thought we were cool ... well, at least she had called my baby cute ...* I thought then as I do now. Otherwise, I might have entered the room a little differently that day...

"Hey, guys!" I said, announcing my presence. They hadn't known I was there at first, but I had observed Calvin handing Lisa a wad of money and had watched her shove it deep into her purse. I pretended like I hadn't seen it but , of course, took a mental note for later reference with Calvin.

"Uh ... hi, Jay," said Lisa with a smile. "I was just leaving." She brushed past me and headed towards the living room. "I forgot something and had to turn around and come back. Well, I'll see y'all later." She turned back for a moment to give Calvin the eye, meaning she would talk to him later about whatever they had been arguing about. And then she was gone. I turned to look at Calvin, giving him my own evil eye.

"What?" he asked me innocently, walking past me and back into the living room where the TV was on.

"You tell me *what?*" I said in response. "What was all that about?"

"All what?" He found the remote under the couch and went into his mode of flipping channels while we talked.

"Calvin," I said, sighing in exasperation. I hated it when he did that and played guessing games with me. It was very tiring and really pissed me off at times when I was trying to get to the bottom of something. "I heard you guys arguing when I first came in the door. What were you arguing about?"

"Oh, nothin' important. Just a little family rivalry, that's all."

"Hmm ... didn't sound like that to me. You guys were pretty intense back there. And how much money did you give her?"

"Oh, here we go with this shit again," he said, rolling his eyes and throwing the remote down on the coffee table. "Why, Jaycee? Does it really matter? I told you, she's family, and as long as we're stayin' here under her roof, we have to hold our own. Don't you understand that?"

"I understand that perfectly fine, but why do you have to keep shelling out so much money to her like you're her pimp daddy or something?" This amused him and he started laughing uncontrollably.

"Wow, Jay. That was pretty good," he said.

"Well, it's true, Calvin. You keep going like you're doing, and we're going to run out of money, and then what are we going to do? Huh? How are we supposed to get to California with no money?" There, I had finally said it and felt relieved. He was silent and squinted his eyes at the TV like he was really trying to concentrate on the show that was playing. I grabbed the remote and turned it off.

"Calvin?!"

"What, girl?!" He gave me a very annoying look, but I had captured his attention. He hated it when I turned the TV off while he was watching it, which was why I took pleasure in doing it. In the little time we had known each other, I was still amazed at how we had learned how to utterly disgust one another just as well as we could please each other.

"How much money do we have left?"

"Man, Iono — why? I told you I would take care of you, so what are you trippin' for?"

"Because you act like you hit the lottery or something and have millions of dollars to just throw away. And I know that money has to run out sooner or later, the way you're going through it, and I'm afraid we're going to run out before we get to California."

"Don't worry, Jaycee. We have plenty of money to go

around. And anyway, my pops finally sent that other money I told you about when we first met, so that's what you saw me give Lisa. He is her uncle, you know, so some of it was for her."

"Oh," I said. I guess that made sense then. I suddenly felt bad for antagonizing him. "So, how much do we have altogether now?" I asked, intrigued by the nonstop cash flow that seemed to come our way. For the first time, I wondered what his father did for a living — and if it was anything remotely close to his son's career … or lack thereof.

* * * * *

Come to think of it, I began to wonder what exactly it was that the whole Jones clan did for a living. We were heading into the month of May, which meant that it was still pretty chilly and Lisa was always wearing those skimpy little outfits under her long, leather trench coat. They were cute for the figure she had, and a little too risqué for my taste, but highly too revealing for an office job. All Calvin had told me was that she was an assistant for a very high profile black businessman, and that he liked his female employees to dress that way for the clients. Lisa never mentioned her job, except that she was very tired from it when she came home. She would always head straight for the bathroom, too, and take long hot showers, but then I had done the same every evening when I had come home after a long, hard day. It was very relaxing. I would always fix her a nice cup of hot tea that would be waiting for her when she got out … like the good housemaid I was.

I had half a mind to make her and Calvin start paying me for my services so I could join in all of the cash giveaways. Between combing the girls' hair, keeping the house clean and preparing the daily meals, I was turning into the average nanny ... and love-slave for my new husband. It was sort of an unspoken thing, but now sex between us was as regular as ever, and part of my daily regimen along with all of the other chores. I had no complaints there, though. I enjoyed it as much as he did and looked forward to our sheet sessions.

* * * * *

He never did answer my question about the money, but I dismissed it for the moment and decided to bring up the part about me and C.J. not being a part of their plan.

"Calvin?"

"Now what?" he sighed.

"I overheard Lisa talking to you about a plan? What did she mean by that?"

"Huh?" he asked with a stupid look on his face.

"Some plan that apparently C.J. and I were not supposed to be a part of. Just what did she mean by that?" I asked indignantly, with my hands on my hips.

"Oh, she didn't mean no harm," he said, laughing it off and shooing the topic away with his hand as if he were swatting a fly.

"Well, what did she mean by it?" I pressed him.

"See, I stayed here with her for awhile before I went to Kansas ..."

"Mm-hmm," I said, sitting back down on the couch beside him.

"And money was kind of tight for me, so she hooked me up with this gig with one of her boss' friends, and they sent me on this run that was supposed to last about three days. I was supposed to come back when it was done, then I met you." *Gig. I knew what that meant. So, he had been dealing drugs the whole time. He never stopped, like he had led on when we met.* It was all coming together now. And I had kind of messed things up for Ms. Lisa, it appeared. Oh, I bet she was a getting a bigger pleasure than I thought from me running around her house ragged all day, trying to keep things in order. It was all payback for her. And Calvin had gone along with the whole thing without even letting on. Suddenly, I felt used.

"Oh," I said.

"Oh? That's all you have to say?" he asked, a little disappointed. "Well, ain't you glad we met?" I didn't quite know how to answer that one, but I was sure to choose my words carefully.

"Well ... yeah. I'm glad I have C.J., but Calvin, it was never my plan to fall in love and marry a drug dealer. You lied to me ... you've been lying to me from the very beginning ... our whole relationship has just been one big lie."

"How is that? I never lied about nothin'. I did stop dealin' for awhile. Then, I just started back up again and didn't tell you right away."

"Not saying anything is the same thing as lying, Calvin," I said. "No wonder you never wanted to get a real job. No wonder you're always so scared of cops. Now it all makes sense. Calvin, what else do I need to know about you? Just let me know, now, because I'm tired of all these little surprises ... they're getting real old ..."

"So what? What are you tryin' to say? You want a divorce, now?"

"Did I say that?" I shot back. "Boy, you're awful quick to resort to that every time we have a little disagreement? But will we really need to get one, now that you mention it?"

"Where are you going with that?" he asked me.

"Well, I don't know. Damn, I'm wondering if the next story I hear is that Lisa's not really your cousin, and she's actually your first wife — and those are really your daughters instead of your second cousins! It really wouldn't surprise me with all of the other crap I've been finding out here lately."

"What?!" Calvin exclaimed. "Girl, what are you smokin'?" I knew that remark was absurd, but I was truly serious. I couldn't put anything past him now and wondered if I could ever trust him. We had only been married a little over a month, now and we had already had two major fights over trust.

Exasperated over the whole ordeal, I threw my hands up in the air and went to check on C.J. He was awake, lying in the center of the bed with pillows encased around him like a padded fortress. His little feet were kicking in the air uncontrollably. He would be six months old in a couple of days, and his little features were changing daily, becoming more and more defined, and looking more and more like Calvin. I picked him up, and as I held him, I wondered what else his father had in store for us in the next two days. I was beginning to think I had married a chameleon with ever-changing spots … just when I think I had him figured out, he would switch up on me again. I didn't know how much more I could take. I wept silently in frustration. This was not the life I had dreamt for myself.

Chapter Fourteen

THE PHONE RANG, waking me up. I must have dozed while I was putting C.J. back to sleep after his feeding. I laid him back down and went into the kitchen to answer it.

"Hello?"

"Hey," it was Lisa.

"Hey," was all I could muster. I felt like cussing her out, but knew better. I couldn't afford for us to be out in the streets with no place to go, and I wasn't too keen on going back to a motel.

"Whatcha doin'?"

"Nothin'. I just woke up. I must have fallen asleep with the baby."

"Must be nice. We can trade places anytime," she said, laughing. Her laugh was always warm and inviting, encouraging you to laugh with her. It was easy to believe she and Calvin were related. They both had a way of melting me down even when I was mad at them.

"Did you want to talk to Calvin?" I asked, looking around for him. I assumed that's why she was calling. I hadn't noticed him in the living room, and all was quiet throughout the apartment.

"Naw. Actually, I called to talk to you. He's probably not there anyway." I was going to ask how she knew that, but she answered for me. "He called me a little while ago and told me what happened between you two. I was just calling to apologize. Don't blame him, Jay. That was all my fault. I didn't know you had come back and overheard us talking, but I shouldn't have said those things about you and the baby. I'm sorry."

"So where did he go?"

"He said he was gonna go hang out with some of his boys and give you a chance to cool off."

"Oh. Well, you don't have anything to be sorry about. He's the one that misled me and keeps lying about everything, not you."

"He means well. He just wants everybody to love him, and will say and do whatever it takes to make that happen."

"Lisa, love comes from trusting someone. I can't trust someone who doesn't tell the truth, and I can't love someone who I can't trust."

"So, what are tryin' to say?" she asked, a little on the defensive side.

"I'm not trying to say anything more or anything less. I'm just trying to make a point."

"Point taken," she said, though I doubted it. "Jaycee, remember what we talked about? Sometimes men do and say stupid shit to get us and keep us. They don't know no better. And most of the time, they mean well. I really like you, and I think you'll be good for Calvin. He does need to grow up a bit, but he needs you to be there for him. You're strong and honest and that's what he needs. He can't do it without you." Boy, was she making it hard for a sister. Even, if I had wanted to leave Calvin, I couldn't now, not with his cousin earnestly begging me to stick by him — and complimenting me all in the same breath. "Besides, I need you, too. Whose gonna keep my house clean after you're gone?"

"Unh," I grunted, and we both started laughing. We chatted for awhile about this and that, then I heard a man in the background and Lisa told me she had to go.

I looked at the clock and it was nearing one o'clock. There were a few dishes in the sink left over from breakfast and the night before, so I started some hot water to begin soaking them. Lisa had a dishwasher, but I liked doing them the old-fashioned way, like my grandmother had taught me. I reflected on what Lisa had said and tried to convince myself that she was right and that Calvin did need me get his life together and turn things around. I really did love him and wanted the best for all of us. I was also still fighting the pride factor and was not quite ready to give in and head back home no matter how ugly things got ... not just yet. I owed it to Calvin and myself to stick things out. I owed it to our son.

Finally, Calvin came strolling in shortly after I had finished cleaning the bathroom and straightening the living room up. He looked awful. His skin had a gray shade to it and he was sweating profusely, and his eyes had that filmy look again, like they were that night in the motel. He looked like he had been running from a pack of dogs or something ... or maybe the cops. At any rate, I was afraid to ask. He walked right past me like he didn't even see me and went into the bedroom. I figured he was going to lie down, then I thought about it and panicked, bolting down the hall to catch him before he landed on our son, figuring he might not see him either. When I entered the room, C.J. was in the same spot I had left him, untouched. I found Calvin passed out cold on the floor, beside the bed. I frowned as I reached for a pillow, but was relieved to find our son still intact and unharmed. I took the pillow and gently placed it under Calvin's head and threw a blanket over him. I opted to let him sleep off whatever it was ailing him, although I felt like throwing a pitcher of cold water on him to wake him up. As soon as he did wake up, we were going to the store to purchase a portable crib for C.J. I couldn't risk another episode like that again. But he never did awaken, at least not on his own.

* * * * *

Lisa came home early that day and told me not to worry about picking up the girls from the bus stop. She had already taken care of them and had found a sitter for them who lived just a couple of doors down from us. She was even going to watch C.J., but for what, I didn't know. I didn't feel like partying, and it was only Wednesday.

"What's up with the babysitter?" I asked, getting C.J.'s diaper bag together.

"Where's Calvin?" she asked, looking around a little frantic.

"He's sleeping on the floor in the bedroom. Why, what's wrong?" I asked, following her into the bedroom.

"How long has he been asleep?" she grabbed his arm, checking for a pulse, it seemed. "Shit!"

"What?!" Suddenly, I was hysterical.

"How long has he been asleep, Jay?"

"I don't know. A couple of hours, I guess. Why? Is he ... dead?" I could feel my heart thudding hard against my chest as I asked the question.

"No," she answered, relieving herself and me at the same time. "At least not yet, but that' why I got a babysitter. We need to get him to the hospital now," she said, lifting his arms and attempting to sit him up. I dropped the diaper bag and helped her drag him into the living room, holding his legs. She ran into the bathroom and turned the faucet on. She returned with a cold, wet towel. "Here, apply this to his forehead ..." She scared me talking like that, so proper and all, but it sounded very professional, like she had learned it from a line in a movie or something. Instantly, I could tell that she had gone through this before. I was just wondering if it had been with Calvin, but I didn't ask. I didn't really want to know. "... while I take the baby over to Sheila's. I'll be right back."

I sat next to Calvin and applied the towel like Lisa had said and tried talking to Calvin, hoping he'd hear me and wake up. I put my head against his chest to make sure his heart was still beating, and was relieved to hear that it was, though faintly.

"C'mon, Lisa," I whined. "Hurry up!" As if on cue, the door flew open and Lisa charged over with two guys behind her. They lifted him off the couch as if he were a feather and took him down to the car while Lisa and I followed closely behind. We thanked them both and hurried on to the hospital. I sat in the back and carefully followed Lisa's instructions. About every five seconds, she would yell back at me to check his pulse or heartbeat to make sure he was still with us, and each time I dreaded doing it, fearing the worst. His head rested in my lap while he lay there unconscious, completely oblivious to everything that was going on around him. It was all I could do to keep from going into hysterics and hyperventilating myself, but I knew that Lisa would flip if I lost it. She needed me as much as I needed her to remain in control ... for Calvin's sake.

We arrived at the emergency room after what seemed like hours, but in actuality it had only been about ten or fifteen minutes, the way Lisa was driving through traffic, ignoring red lights and stop signs. She had put us all near death, but it was a good thing, the doctor had said, because "... another five minutes would have cost Calvin *his life.*" I shuddered at the thought, still in bewilderment about the whole ordeal. I wanted to know what was going on. *What was wrong with Calvin when he had first come home earlier this afternoon? Why had he acted so strange? Why did he lose consciousness?*

Lisa answered all of my questions later on that night after we left Calvin at the hospital for *further observations* and went home to get the kids and put them in bed. Since I couldn't give Calvin the third degree, I couldn't wait to lay into Lisa. I took a quick shower, and this time there was a cup of hot tea waiting for me when I got out.

"I just have one question for starters," I said, plopping down onto the couch beside her and reaching for my cup.

"Shoot," she said, ready and willing.

"How did you know to come home for Calvin? How did you know something was wrong?"

"That was two questions," she said, smiling, not amusing me at all. When she saw the look I gave her, she cleared her throat and straightened her pose like she was in trouble. "Umm ... I got a page from one of Calvin's friends, and they told me that he had gone too far with some smoke and that I might wanna go home and keep an eye on him."

"Smoke?"

"You know, the pipe." I was still none the wiser as I looked at her and frowned.

"My grandpa used to smoke a pipe and he never passed out or got sick from it." Apparently, I had told a joke without realizing it, making Lisa chuckle. She was pissing me off with her nonchalance about the whole thing, and she must have sensed my intolerance with her because she stopped laughing.

"Why do you keep laughing at me?"

"Because I didn't know you were so ignorant to all of this. You don't have a clue what I'm talkin' about, do you?"

"No," I admitted.

"Well, let me make it plain, then. Calvin O.D.'d today. You do know what that means, don't you?"

"Yeah, he overdosed. On what?"

"Crack."

"Crack? But that's a drug."

"Good girl," said Lisa. "You're catching on." I was not amused by her sarcasm in the least.

"Calvin doesn't use drugs," I said, laughing, "he deals them. There's a big difference."

"Yeah, there should be a big difference, but not with Calvin. It just makes it easy for him to get access to it. I thought he had straightened up and quit that shit, but apparently not."

"Whoa! What do you mean quit? Are you trying to tell me that Calvin has done this before? That he's a drug addict?"

"You're not jivin', are you?" she answered me with a question, and my heart sank. "You mean, Calvin never told you? You didn't know?" I shook my head no and slumped down in the corner of the couch. I was devastated and felt like overdosing on something myself, just to get out of my reality check. I immediately went into a shell and blocked out everything else she said.

"Jay? Jay? Snap out of it?" I came to from my stupor and looked at Lisa. She was kneeling down in front of me, waving her hands in my face, trying to get my attention. "You all right?" she asked me, getting off her knees and joining me on the couch. I sat back up and wiped my face. Apparently I had been crying without even realizing it. Lisa handed me a Kleenex off the coffee table and I blew my nose. "You okay, Jay?" Her voice was very subdued and she looked genuinely concerned, despite her flippancy with me earlier. I nodded my head in response, not really feeling like talking.

"Look, I know this must come as a shock to you," she

said. *Who are you telling?* I thought to myself. "And I'm sorry, I truly am. I thought you knew about Calvin's past. I figured he told you, but I guess not since he couldn't even tell you the truth about where he was from."

"Hmph," I grunted, reflecting on that lie.

"Try not to be so hard on him, Jaycee. He really needs you now more than ever …"

"Ex-cuse me?" I pumped up. *"Try not to be so hard on him?* How can you say that, Lisa? He totally misled me. For Christ's sake, I'm married to a drug addict? How do you think that makes me feel right about now? Huh? He has not only lied to me about everything under the sun, but he's put my whole life in jeopardy since I met him, and now our son's. Our son could have been born addicted to that stuff?"

"Not likely, Jay. Usually, it takes more of the mother's addiction to have any real impact on the baby. And since you're clean, there's only a minute percentage that C.J. was affected at all." I almost hit the roof when I heard her say *minute*, sounding all professional and what not, like she was a real doctor or expert on the matter.

"Well, I don't give a damn how *minute* the percentage is or could have been. There was still a risk, and Calvin had no business getting involved with me — or furthermore having a baby with me without letting me know about his … drug addiction." Every time I had to mention his condition, a lump formed in my throat. I resented even the thought of Calvin's whole condition, much less having to talk about it aloud. Lisa grabbed my arm, trying to comfort me, but to no avail. I was growing tired of her excuses for Calvin as much as I had had enough of his lies.

" Jay, I know you're mad."

Damn, right I'm mad! I fumed silently.

"I can't apologize enough for my cousin."

It will never be enough!

"Just, please, try to look at Calvin's side of things. He only lied to you because he really loved you."

"Unh," I grunted again. *Now, that was original*, I thought. "You call that love, Lisa?"

"Yes, I really do." I looked at her and knew that she meant it, but it still didn't wash.

"Well, I don't. I call it manipulation … and betrayal."

"How did Calvin betray you?"

"Because he told me that he would never do anything to harm me or C.J., that he would always put us first above any — and everything, and that we would always be number one in his life. Well, we're not … his little habit is." Lisa sighed and leaned back on the couch. I was wearing her out just as much as she was me.

"Well, baby girl, life doesn't always turn out the way we intend."

"Hmph, ain't that the truth," I agreed. We sat in mutual stupor for what seemed like hours, just sipping on our tea and reflecting on the days' events in our own minds. Then, I finally broke the silence.

"Lisa?"

"Yeah."

"Did you know that Calvin was back on drugs?" I asked.

"No. Honest. I didn't. At least, not right away. That's the first thing I asked him when he called and asked me could y'all crash here for a minute. He knows I don't play that shit. I got enough issues of my own without adding on an extra burden like that." I nodded in agreement, satisfied with her answer … almost anyway.

"Would you have told me if you had known for sure?"

"Probably not," she admitted, surprising me a little.

"Why not?" I inquired, turning around to face her and crossing my legs, Indian style.

"Because like I told you before, Jaycee. I don't get in people's business like that. It causes more problems than the problem itself. And what if I had been wrong and stirred up trouble for nothin'. Then y'all both would have been swole at me. Sometimes it's best to leave well enough alone in a situation like that. Believe me, the truth always has a way of comin' out of the darkness in due time. And anyway, would you have really believed me if I had tried to tell you?" I thought about her question.

"Well, no, probably not. Calvin was pretty good at hiding it up until now. I guess the fact that he dealt drugs, too, was a good camouflage because if I ever found anything, he could always say it was for his clients."

"Right."

"And he always had a load of money, so how would I have known?"

"He always kept money because he was skimmin' on the product and selling it anyway like it was all still intact."

"Really?" I asked. Then, I drew a vivid flashback of the morning his boss, Mr. Rawlins, busted in our apartment, looking for his money. He must have caught on to what Calvin had been doing, and that's why he was so intense, putting it lightly.

"So, that explains it," I said, matter of factly.

"That explains what?" Lisa asked, inquisitively.

"That morning we got a surprise visit from his boss, Mr. Rawlins."

"What happened?" Lisa turned around to face me now, and mocked me, crossing her legs the same way I had mine. We looked like a couple of teenagers with our heads together, sitting up in the middle of the night, sharing our innermost secrets. I began to rehash that terrible morning, telling her everything that had transpired.

When I had finished, she was speechless. Then, just like that, she became outraged.

"What the hell is wrong with that boy? Putting y'all in danger like that! He knows better than that shit! Y'all could've been killed!" *Duh*, I was thinking, but sat quietly, letting her fume. I was a little relieved to know someone finally shared my sentiments about the whole thing.

"We have to get him some help," I said. "Is there a rehab center around here or something that he can go to when he comes out of the hospital?"

"Tsk," Lisa clucked her tongue loudly. "If that's what you wanna call it. Honey, them places don't work. And, anyway, the good ones are all out of town. I think the closest one that's worth checking out is down south a little ways, in Oklahoma City. But, really they're all the same. He has to wanna help himself, first of all." She was right about that. I would come to find that out, shortly.

Chapter Fifteen

CALVIN WAS RELEASED from the hospital three days later, but under the conditions that he would immediately check into a drug rehab. I was relieved to know that I wouldn't have to twist his arm about it because he had no choice. Surprisingly, he didn't fight the matter and willingly agreed. I guess the fact that he almost died must have really opened his eyes to some things.

So our trip to California was delayed for a few months, as Calvin was to initially stay for thirty days, then sixty days if the first time failed, then ninety days after his second admittance. And after that, he could wind up staying anywhere from six months to a year in rehab. I balked at the absurdity of the terms and conditions. This was actually in writing on a contract that he had to sign in order to be admitted. I couldn't believe it. I thought the whole idea was ludicrous, and it virtually encouraged the addicts to keep coming back, as if it were a bed and breakfast that they could come crash at anytime they wanted ... as long as they promised to hang around long enough to try all the different varieties of brunch choices.

Lisa had also informed me on the night that we shared, there was no more money. That's what Calvin and she had been arguing about the morning I walked in on them. She had suspected he was doing something when he began stalling on giving her some money that he promised her, and confronted him about it. All in all,

Calvin had wound up smoking up at least five thousand dollars worth of crack that we knew of and probably more than that since he had never been straight with me or Lisa on how much he had acquired from the beginning, back in Kansas. He had led her to believe that we had blown most of it on our honeymoon, and I, in turn, thought he had been giving it all to her. He had bamboozled both of us.

* * * * *

"That's what crackheads do," Lisa had bluntly informed me. "They lie and lie, then lie and lie, and lie some more to keep covering up the previous lie. They lie to get into shit, then lie to get out of it." I shuddered at the depiction, and every time she said *crackhead*, I twinged. I abhorred having any relationship to that label. I was now a co-dependent to a crackhead ... what a title to have. A nicer word that people liked to use was *addict*, but to me it was all the same. No matter how they wanted to sugarcoat it, I was still offended that I had to be called anything relating to the matter other than Calvin's *wife*, and the whole ordeal was quite belittling.

* * * * *

As part of the rules and regulations, I was not allowed to talk to Calvin or visit him while he was in rehab, but we were allowed to correspond by letter. I think I received a letter every day of the week after the first week he was in there. I wasn't even aware that Calvin could form a complete sentence on paper, until then. He wrote about missing me and promising me that this would never happen again, and that he would get a real job once he got out. He was going to come back refreshed and "renewed in his spirit," he said. Apparently, the rehab had this *Twelve Steps* program which highly encouraged a relationship with God or some spiritual being in order to fully reap the benefits of sincerely changing and turning your life around as an addict. Thus, he was forever quoting scriptures from the Bible. He was truly inspiring at times and probed me to seek my own spirituality, and I eventually found a little Baptist church near the apartment that I would attend occasionally. I tried to get Lisa to go with me, but she wanted no part of it, claiming that all *saints* were hypocrites. But sometimes she would let her two older daughters tag along in case I got the spirit and needed help with C.J., which happened every now and then.

Once I knew that there was no money left, I grew frantic and decided to go job hunting. Sheila, Lisa's neighbor from down the hall, proved to be a godsend and agreed to babysit C.J. during the day for me for free. I promised her that as soon as I got on my feet, I would start paying her, but she insisted on not charging me, claiming that she had been in my shoes once and knew how it was, being left alone with a kid while your husband dried out somewhere. So I surrendered and began my search.

There weren't many jobs to choose from with the kind of degree that I had unless I wanted to be a substitute schoolteacher. I hadn't completed my education, so my options were limited. Had I majored in Business or something more practical, I could have found an office job or something. I got a lot of free advice to go back to school, but, of course, that wasn't one of my options at the moment. I needed a job to make ends meet *now*, not later.

After three weeks of day in and day out searching for a job, I had resorted to either retail or fast food, not really wanting to do either, but would settle for retail if I had to. Then, one day Lisa candidly suggested that I come apply at her job. Her offer took me by surprise, since I had mentioned before that she never talked about her job to any great lengths or detail. I was drinking a can of soda when we had begun the conversation and when I finally asked her just what it is that she did, I almost choked in horror ... she worked for an escort service.

"Excuse me?"

"What?" she asked, innocently.

"I just know I didn't hear you right. What did you say you do?" I asked again, hoping to hear something differently.

"I said, I'm an escort." *Well, that explains all the skimpy attire*, I thought to myself.

"And what exactly does that mean?" I asked, not wanting to entertain any mixed ideas I had parading through my head.

"My boss sends me on ... *executive meetings* with professional businessmen," she said, smiling as if she were trying to convince herself of her job description and was pleased with the explanation.

"In other words, you mean he sends you on dates to have sex with men who have white-collar jobs," I said. Lisa looked at me with one raised eyebrow and gave me a devilish grin.

"One could look at it that way," she said, smoothing her mini-skirt out and adjusting her breasts in the top she was wearing that was two sizes too small — but looked fantastic. I shook my head in disgust, not believing my ears. "Well, I don't always have sex with them," she said, trying to clean it up. "Only if they're fine," she said cunningly.

"Unh," I grunted. "I don't think AIDS has any criteria," I said.

"Girl, I use condoms!" she exclaimed. I rolled my eyes at her in dismay. As if that made things more acceptable.

"Lisa," I sighed. "How do you do it?" She looked at me and laughed.

"You know what I mean," I said. "How do you sleep at night, knowing what you've done all day? How do you look at your daughters?" I had gone too far with my questions, and knew it as soon as I'd said it, but I was only being honest with her.

"Huh," she scowled. "My job has nothin' to do with my daughters, okay? And where do you get off judgin' me, Little Miss High and Mighty? Don't you ever question my motherhood with what I do for a livin'," she said, waving her finger at me and rolling her neck, sister style. "One has nothin' to do with the other, okay. And don't you forget that!"

"I'm sorry, Lisa," I said, "that's not what I meant ..."

"Then you need to clarify," she said with her hands on her hips.

"I didn't mean that you were a bad mother. What I meant was ... aren't you afraid that your daughters might want to do what you do when they grow up? I mean, you're the one that always talks about making a good life for your girls and seeing that they have the best of everything, and ..."

"And that's what the hell I'm doin'," she said, matter of factly. "Do you know how much I get paid for what I do? The money's damn good. And like I told you, I'm not a prostitute — I don't *have* to have sex if I don't choose to. It's my call. Half the time, the men are older and just want a little company for dinner or whatever. They're mostly older and couldn't probably get it up if they wanted to. They have money to throw away, and if that's what they want to do, then, shit, I'll stand there — or lay there when the mood hits me — and catch it." And with that, she got up from the kitchen table we had been sitting at and stomped off to her bedroom, high heels and all.

 I slumped back in my chair and reflected on the conversation we had just had and was still in shock over the whole episode. I couldn't believe what all I had encountered in the past six months ... first finding out that my husband was a drug addict, now knowing that my cousin-in-law was a call girl. I could feel my grandmother kicking the top of her casket now, trying to pry it open so that she could come give me a swift kick. I knew my parents would disown me if they ever found out. They practically had already ... or worse, they might have tried to take C.J. away from me and prove me unfit. I could see my mother doing that. I shuddered at the thought and went to bed myself.

 I stopped by Lisa's bedroom and tapped on the door lightly, but she had either gone to sleep or had decided she wasn't talking to me. At any rate, I vowed to make amends with her in the morning, and to my surprise, contemplated taking her up on her offer — or at least finding out more about it and seeing if I could get around the whole sex thing. I could tolerate the dating stuff, but did not want to go any further than the dinners. I couldn't believe that I was even considering such a thing, but I had to make some money somehow. And I had to make a lot of it pretty fast.

 As soon as Calvin was out of rehab, I wanted to get him as far away from this town as possible. Lisa had promised she wouldn't tell him, and I believed her. It was her idea after all, so I could always put it back on her if he ever did find out. I convinced myself that it wouldn't be cheating, as long as I didn't have sex with them, it would just be making ends meet, like Lisa, but on a much lower level — or higher, depending on how you looked at it.

Chapter Sixteen

THE NEXT MORNING, I tried talking to Lisa, but she kept ignoring me like I wasn't even talking to her. But she would smile and coo at C.J. just to spite me, who was right there in my arms. I took the silent abuse with grace and pretended it didn't bother me, although it did.

After sleeping on the matter and praying earnestly the night before, chanting Romans 8:28 ... *"and we know that all things work together ..."* over and over in my head, I waived Lisa's offer and decided to try God one more time. I was determined to live right and find a job and get my family out of dodge, if it killed me. The money sounded damn good, but like Grandma always said, *"All money ain't good money,"* and after being involved with Calvin Jones, I knew that to be, oh, so true. I also recalled one of my mother's favorite sayings she liked to use when she didn't like my choice in friends ... *"If you stay around a barber shop long enough, you'll wind up getting a haircut."* I never quite understood her until just recently, but when I finally did, it rang in my ears, crystal clear.

I finished feeding C.J. and put him in his carrier to get ready to go. On my way out I stopped in the doorway and looked at Lisa, who was standing in the kitchen, pouring a cup of coffee.

"Um, Lisa. Thanks for the offer, but I think I'll pass on the haircut this time," I said and smiled. She turned around and gave me a very puzzled look, and I just laughed and walked out the door. I left and dropped C.J. off at Sheila's and began my daily venture.

After weighing my options of whether I wanted to flip burgers or dress up mannequins, I decided to try my hand at a local boutique around the corner from the apartment. It was close enough to home that I could still drop in and check on C.J. on my lunch hour, and stop by the apartment and fix myself a sandwich, so I wouldn't be spending any extra money on fast food. I was still trying to lose weight from having C.J., so the last thing I needed was to start having hamburgers and French fries every day of the week. And I opted for walking instead of wasting gas in the car.

I was hired on the spot, to my surprise. The manager was a petite older white lady in her late thirties, maybe early forties, but dressed and acted like she was holding onto twenty-nine for the life of her. Her hair was dyed a natural blonde, although her roots told a different story, and she wore it long, cascading over her thin, over-tanned shoulders. Although I could see early signs of wrinkles around the corners of her eyes, her make-up was flawless.

She welcomed the fact that I wasn't a local applicant and was very impressed that I had *some college*. It was a predominantly Black and Latino neighborhood where we lived, and she admitted that she had fired numerous girls before me for letting their friends come in and rob her blind. During the interview, I boldly asked her why she hadn't relocated, *surely she could have done well in her own neck of the woods*. She had agreed with me, but mentioned that the taxes were cheaper in *our neighborhood* for lot space, and that her shop was actually on the edge, bordering between our neighborhood and hers, so that she was still able to attract *her people*, too. Any other Black person might have been offended by her comments and reasoning, but it actually made perfect sense to me. And since my only concern was finding a decent job with clean money, I didn't care what she did with her business or the why and the how, I was just grateful she liked me for whatever reason and wanted me to work for her.

Once Lisa found out where I worked, she softened a bit and began talking to me again. Eventually, she got around to asking me if she could she use my discount to get some new clothes, which I had figured she would and, of course, I said yes. So we were buddies again, and since I had a job also, we took turns preparing meals and making hot tea at night for each other once the kids were all tucked in.

* * * * *

Thirty days flew by, and before I knew it, it was time to pick up Calvin. I had actually grown accustomed to him not being around to call the shots and issue me money when he felt I needed it. I had even taken it upon myself to go to the office of the apartment complex and filled out an application for a two-bedroom apartment of our own. I opted for a six-month lease instead of the year-lease, figuring six months was enough time to save enough money and start our lives over again. Also, Calvin had promised to find a job, too, so with both of our incomes coming in, we would be on our way to California in no time.

Sheila babysat again while Lisa and I went to pick up Calvin. The ride to Oklahoma City was kind of quiet, as we were both anxious to see Calvin, but nervous at the same time. We had both sat up the night before, talking about ways we could work together to make sure that Calvin didn't have a relapse. She tried to discourage me from moving out, thinking that would be a big mistake, but I assured her that we would be fine, and only two floors underneath her, so I really didn't see the big deal. Being so close, it really wasn't much of a difference than if we lived in a split-level house. She didn't like it, but backed down nonetheless.

Calvin, on the other hand, seemed very sure of himself and had enough confidence for us all. His color was back to that coffee brown that I loved so much, and his spirits seemed definitely renewed. Whatever fears I had slowly went away, and I was just thankful that I had my husband back in one lively piece. It was time we got our life and our marriage back on track. We were still considered newlyweds, but had already experienced at least ten years worth of "for better or worse." I myself was ready to get on with the better.

We stayed with Lisa for one more week, and then our apartment was ready for us to move in. Susan, my boss, had just bought some new furniture and offered to sell me her old set for little or nothing. It was a black leather sofa and loveseat with a matching recliner, and I thought she was out of her mind because it still looked like new to me, but I jumped on the deal, afraid to pass it up. She said she was tired of black and wanted a brighter look in her home. I was thrilled because it reminded me of my old living room that I had furnished back home, which had been outfitted in black and gold.

Calvin found a job flipping burgers and, at last, we were on our way to getting back to normal, with both of us working and taking care of home. He found an AA meeting to go to on Tuesday and Thursday evenings, and I went with him the first couple of times. He even started attending church with me, and after only three visits he surprised me by standing up and joining. It was a very emotional time for me, and I was so taken aback, I almost forgot to get up and follow him down the aisle to shake the pastor's hand. We rededicated our lives to God and had C.J. baptized the following Sunday. He was still an infant, going on eight months, so actually all they did was sprinkle a few drops of water on his forehead. It was still eventful, and the only thing I regretted was that my parents weren't there to see.

With a little coaxing and some help from Calvin, I even got Lisa to go to church with us from time to time, and although she never joined, she would still send the girls to Sunday school with us, and she eventually stopped working for the escort service. She found a job as a receptionist for a dating service — legitimate dating, and we both laughed when she told me, knowing what I was thinking, but I was happy for her all the same ... happy for us all. Things were finally looking up for the Jones clan.

Then one day Calvin neglected to pick me up from work, and when I walked home to see if he had possibly forgotten and fell asleep, he was nowhere to be found. He got off work an hour earlier than I did, so oftentimes he would grab a quick shower or short snooze before picking me up. I argued with him about walking home, enjoying the opportunity to get in some exercise, but he had refused, saying no wife of his had to walk anywhere. Instead, he went and bought me one of those exercise bicycles that sat in the corner of our bedroom along with his weights. We had thought about moving into a three-bedroom in order to make an exercise room, but then I reminded him that our stay in Oklahoma was supposed to be short-lived. As short as I could make it.

I went upstairs and checked to see if he had gone up to get C.J. from Sheila's, but he was not there either. I asked her to keep C.J. a little while longer while I tried to find him, and she conceded, giving me that pitiful eye that I chose to ignore. I knew what she was thinking and had thought of it myself for a split-second, but dismissed it, hoping for the best.

My only resort was to go down the hall and see if he was at Lisa's, and I as pounded on the door, I prayed that he was there. There was no answer, and I looked at my watch. It was only five-thirty and Lisa didn't usually get home until six. I ran back downstairs, hoping I'd find him at home, but he wasn't there. I threw down my purse in the living room and headed straight for the bedroom, frantically searching the drawers in our dresser, hoping to find some telephone numbers of Calvin's friends. I lucked out and found a couple of numbers to names I had heard him mention before, but neither one had seen him around. I checked the caller I.D., but there were no traces toward Calvin's possible whereabouts.

I changed my clothes into some jeans and tennis shoes, not even bothering to shower, and charged back upstairs to Lisa's, taking the steps two at a time. When I reached her apartment, I was completely out of breath and could only tap faintly on the door. She must have seen me coming, because the door flew open before my hand even touched it. She pulled me in gently by the arm and sat me down on the couch.

"He's gone off and done it again, hasn't he?" she asked.

"How do you know?"

"Sheila called me, worried about you, and left a message for me to go downstairs and check on you as soon as I got home."

"Oh," I said, relieved to know that there was a slight chance we were all wrong about Calvin … but not likely.

"So, where do we start looking?" I asked. "Did anybody page you again this time?"

"No," she said. "Unfortunately, not. He must have found some new friends to hang with on his job."

"Great," I said, frowning. "He can't even go to work

and earn a living without being enticed by that shit. It's everywhere." I was coming to despise the mere mentioning of the word crack, let alone the drug and all of its elements. I couldn't even say it without getting hives, it seemed. It was truly becoming an epidemic in my household and a phenomenal plague all over the country. "Lisa, what are we going to do?" I asked desperately, starting to cry.

"Nothing," she said defiantly. I looked at her, puzzled.

"What do you mean, nothing? We have to do something. You remember what happened the last time, don't you? Calvin almost died. We can't let that happen."

"Jay, Calvin is just gonna have to learn on his own. If we keep bailing him out every time he falls, he's just going to keep doing it and stay on that stuff that much longer." I was horrified at her reasoning, no matter how right she might have been.

"Lisa, we can't just let him die! I can't — he's my husband, for crying out loud! I have to help him!" I went into hysterics, and Lisa had to grab me by the shoulders and shake me to calm me down.

"Jaycee, baby, you have got to get a grip." I turned away from her and tried to shrug away from her firm grip, but she wouldn't let me go. "No! You look at me. Look at me, girl." Her voice cracked, and I looked at her and saw tears in her own eyes. "Now, don't you think for one minute that I don't love that boy as much as you do, if not more. You forget, we go way back. We're family. I know he's your husband and all, but we're blood first, and I love him with all my heart. But Calvin's gotta grow up some time in his life and take some responsibility. You keep this up and he's gonna run you down right along with him."

"Unh-unh," I said, shaking my head. "I'm never trying that shit. Never!"

"I didn't mean it that way, Jaycee. I meant that you can't keep letting this get to you like this. I know, that's easier said than done, but you have a baby to look after. And sad enough, but true, you have a son to raise on your own ... with or without Calvin. You gotta make sure you and that baby are taken care of first, before you go traipsin' all over dodge, worryin' about that boy. He'll come home when he comes down off that stuff. Didn't he last time?"

"Yeah, but look what happened. He just barely got home."

"But he did, and that's all that counts. You just keep going to work and church and prayin' and everything will be all right." I couldn't believe Lisa was preaching to me about anything pertaining to church and praying, two things she hardly did herself. "Now, I know I don't go to church as much as I should, or pray a lot like you. But I have my own understandin' with the Man Upstairs. He can hear me talkin' when I need Him and He knows my heart. That's all that matters. God won't put nothin' on Calvin or any of us that we can't handle. Calvin just has to hit rock bottom. And rock bottom doesn't always mean death, Jay."

Damn, had I not known any better, I would have sworn I was listening to my mother, in the flesh. Lisa sounded just like her, and I wondered if maybe some kind of telekinetic thing had transpired and my mother had jumped into her body to send me a message. It was very weird and utterly freaked me out. I stopped crying to laugh at myself for thinking such a foolish thought, and Lisa looked at me, wondering what was so funny.

"You mind letting me in on the joke?" she inquired.

"Oh," I said wiping my face and reaching for a Kleenex to blow my nose. "It's just that you sounded just like my mother for a second. I thought she had taken over your body, like Patrick Swayze did with Whoopie Goldberg in *Ghost*." She looked at me and we both went into hysterics, cracking up.

"Girl, you crazy," she said.

Chapter Seventeen

LISA INVITED ME and C.J. over to spend the night to keep my mind off of Calvin, but, of course, I turned her down, not wanting to miss him slipping in overnight … or getting a chance to slip back out, unsuspected.

He never showed up that night or the next morning. It was four days before I heard from him. Although I was very upset with Calvin, I had called into work sick three days in a row, frantic that I might miss a phone call from him saying he was in jail or worse, in the hospital again. On the third day, I had decided to go back to work after hearing one of Lisa's sermons about going on with my life and that the bills weren't going to pay themselves. She had promised to talk to him once he returned and was just as disgusted as I was that he had pulled such a stunt. This was the first time that Calvin had been gone from home so long. I could handle four hours of absence outside of work — I could even handle an overnighter, but four days was quite a different story.

"Jaycee?" it was Susan, holding the phone.

"Yeah," I said, surprised and nervous at the same time. It could only have been two people — Lisa or Calvin. Sheila never called me at work about C.J. And if it was Lisa, she had to be calling about Calvin.

"It's the phone for you."

"Hello," I said.

"Jay," it was Calvin. "Baby, I'm sorry. I'm so sorry I

haven't called you before now. But I'm home, waiting for you." *Oh joy*, I thought. I was speechless, unsure of what to say that wouldn't sound too confrontational over the phone and have my boss wondering. "I'll come get you at five o'clock."

"No," I said with vigor. "Don't bother. I'll walk like I have been for the past three days."

"Okay," he said, not pressing the issue. I imagined that he knew he had messed up big time and was not about to indulge in my fury. "I'll see you when you get home ..." I hung up in his face without saying goodbye. Fortunately, Susan had encountered a customer, so she hadn't heard my conversation with Calvin on the phone. I sighed, trying to relieve some quickly built-up stress and went over to one of my mannequins to tidy up the outfit. I was never too good at hiding my expressions, which I always hated, and when Susan was finished ringing her customer up, she walked over to me and asked me how I was, picking up on my ill demeanor. I had unintentionally ripped a button off the dress.

"Damn!" I scoffed at myself under my breath, but Susan had heard me.

"Everything all right?" she asked, smiling.

"Uh, yeah," I said, forcing myself to smile back. "Sorry about the button. I'll go get some thread and sew it back on."

"Never mind that," she said, unbuttoning the rest of the dress. "It was time for a change anyhow. Why don't you go grab a bite to eat or something. You look a little pale ..."

"Susan," I replied, looking at her and laughing. "I'm Black, I haven't looked pale a day in my life!" She laughed with me and blushed a little.

"Well, you know what I mean, figure of speech. You look a bit piqued, like you haven't been eating for a couple of days or something." I put my head down to avoid looking at her. She had no idea how right she was. I hadn't eaten a thing since I'd gone home and found Calvin missing four days ago. All I had been able to consume were endless cups of coffee and hot tea, inevitably adding to my sleepless nights.

"I know you've been sick, but you have to stay healthy. Go find some soup or something."

"Okay," I said, not fighting her. I invited the break. It was after one o'clock, and I was feeling a little faint after being on my feet for almost five hours straight without anything in my stomach, not to mention my lack of sleep.

I had been running on pure adrenaline — and caffeine. Just then, I remembered something Lisa told me that her uncle used to say to her, and she had tried to drill it into me, *"You can't live on love, girl!"* I had laughed at the remark, thinking it was a silly thing to say and not understanding her at first, but now it made perfect sense. *Ain't that the truth!* I thought to myself and went into the office to grab my purse. We were finally into the summer months, in the month of July, but I decided I would take Susan's advice and get some soup. It was true that I hadn't eaten in a couple of days, and although I could have devoured a hamburger, order of fries and a strawberry shake on sight, I wasn't sure how my stomach would handle it.

I silently vented about Calvin. *Who does he think he is, popping in and out my life whenever he gets a whim? I am NOT havin' it! I'll even go back home if I have to than stay here and deal with this shit! When I get home, we're going to sit down and really have a heart to heart. I can't take it anymore. He has to go back into the rehab and get some help. Thirty days was not nearly long enough. He needs to stay a lot longer, at least ninety straight days, maybe even the whole six months. I have got to reason with him and make him see what he's doing to himself ... what he's doing to us.*

On my way back to work, I promised myself that I wouldn't let Calvin charm his way out of anything this time. He was so good at that. I was not about to live the rest of my life in fear of drug dealers kicking my door in, looking for Calvin or working myself to death, trying to pay all of the bills and take care of C.J., while Calvin walked around footloose and fancy-free, smoking up all of his paychecks. No matter what had gone down between my parents and me, I knew that they had raised me better than that, *fo sho*, as Calvin would have put it.

I finished the rest of my work day, vowing to stay strong and stand firm with Calvin, once I got home and talked to him. I was so intense, anticipating what I was going to say to him, that I messed up a couple of times while I was ringing up sales for customers. I gave way too much money back to a surprisingly honest customer and overcharged another lady, having to void out the sale and start all over. Fortunately, they were both nice and didn't seem to mind my shortcomings, and Susan had been in the back, unpacking some previously shipped inventory.

* * * * *

I made it home with C.J. around six o'clock, as usual. I had stopped by Lisa's on the way down for a quick pep talk, but she was busy preparing dinner for the girls. She volunteered to join us in a couple of hours after she got them settled, but I was in a hurry to get everything off my chest and didn't want to waste any more precious time. So I asked her to keep C.J. while I talked to Calvin; then there would be no interruptions or excuses for him to dodge conversation, and she complied.

I put the key in the door and almost had a heart attack, being caught off guard by Calvin's anxious disposition. He met me at the door and had it open before I could finish turning the lock. He just stood there smiling, like it was an average day. I rolled my eyes at him in disgust and walked right past him.

"Hey, aren't you gonna speak?" he asked, closing the door and following me into the bedroom. I ignored him and started changing out of my work clothes. "Hey, not so fast," he said, walking up to me and caressing my arm. "I thought we'd have a little dinner first ..." I jerked away from his touch and gave him a look that could kill. He stepped back, inching to the other side of the bed, holding his hands up in the air like an invisible shield. "What's up with you?"

"Don't touch me! You think you can waltz back in here after being gone for so long and act like everything's peachy king and nothing's changed?" I asked. "Well, you got another thing coming, Mr. Jones."

"Whoa! What's with all the ice?" he asked.

"You have to ask?" I replied angrily. "What do you expect after being gone for four fuckin' days!" I exploded without even thinking. I could not hold my temper any longer. I had started cursing again, which meant that he had gone way too far, acting like he was Mr. Innocent.

"I'm sorry," was all he could say. Then he collapsed on the bed and started crying. I was in total shock. I half expected him to walk off and ignore me for flying off the handle at him. He had done it numerous times before in the heat of an argument ... but never this. I couldn't believe it. He was actually sobbing. Suddenly, my ill temper ceased and I sat down beside him and he laid his head down in my lap.

"What am I going to do with you, Calvin?" I asked pitifully.

"I'm sorry. I'm sick. It's not my fault. It's the drug, it's like it took my soul with the first hit, and each time I feen for it, it's really me tryin' to get it back, but I just fall deeper and deeper ..." I stood up abruptly and let his head fall back onto the bed. He sat up and looked at me, a little disoriented.

"You sonofabitch!" I yelled. In an instant, I had turned into a raving maniac. I hadn't cursed in so long ... it almost felt liberating. "Now, if that ain't a crock of shit, I don't know what is! You mean to tell me that you're not going to take any responsibility for this *illness*, as you put it? That it's not your fault, but the drug's? What is it, a magic pipe that just finds you on its own and forces itself into your mouth? Huh?"

"No, I was just tryin' to explain it to you somehow, what it does. You know, it's hard tryin' to fight it off. But it's almost like magic, in a sense, it's like the shit calls my name ... you gotta understand, Jay ..." I threw my hands up in the air, not understanding one iota of his reasoning.

"Unbelievable!" I turned my back on him, tapping my foot. My arms were folded defiantly across my chest. I was trying to keep from slapping him across his face. He just had no idea how postal I was feeling at that moment.

"It's true, and I'm not the only one. Some dudes from the meetin' said the same thing." I whirled around and glared at him.

"So that's it. That's why I haven't been able to find you. You've made some new smoking buddies, huh, through AA? Un-believ-able! You're supposed to go there to get help and you wind up finding more pipe partners!" I was livid with fury. I couldn't believe it. I stormed out of the bedroom and searched the living room, looking for my purse. He got up and followed me.

"Where are you goin'?"

"I'm outta here!" I exclaimed, digging for my car keys. "I can't take this shit anymore ..." my voice cracked as I started sobbing myself. He tried to grab my arm, but I wouldn't let him. I started walking toward the door to leave, and he dashed in front of me and blocked the door so I couldn't get out.

"Wait! You can't just leave …"

"The hell I can't!" I yelled back, trying to shove him out of the way, but he was stronger than me and did not even budge. "Calvin, move! Just get out of my way … get out of my life! I don't need you or this!"

"You don't mean that, Jay."

"The hell I do!" I said, giving up fighting with him and retiring to the couch.

"Jay, I need you to get me through this," he said, walking over to join me. He knelt down on the floor in front of me, grabbing my knees in desperation. "I can't do it alone."

"Hmph," I grunted. "That's funny. You have no problem getting high without me."

"I would never expose you to that. I go off and get high out of respect for you. I could never do that in front of you, Jaycee."

"Okay, now you're really trippin'!" I said, sounding just like him. It was odd how I could go into *"Calvin Mode"* when I was really hot, sounding ghetto, just like him. He had a way of bringing me to his level like that. I imagine that's where all the cursing evolved. He never really cursed as bad as I did, but he would make me so angry that I would lose my religion, so to speak, and wind up talking slang, speaking words and phrases that weren't a part of my normal vocabulary.

"How in the hell do you call what you do *respect?*" I asked, indignantly.

"Because I have enough love for you to not do it in our home or in front of our son."

"You call this a *home?*" I asked.

"Well, we're a family, right?"

"We're supposed to be, but I can't tell by the way you're acting, Calvin."

"Hmph, likewise," he said. "You know, it's been real hard for me since my moms died. I thought you, out of everybody, would understand what I'm goin' through. But I guess not …"

"Oh, don't even," I snapped. "Calvin, that's the lowest of the low. You're wrong for bringing your mother into this. She has nothing to do with this. My grandmother just died not too long ago, and you don't see me strung out on drugs, do you?"

"It's not the same, Jay. She was my mother, not just a grandma I saw every now and then."

"It doesn't matter, Calvin. Mother, grandmother, sister, brother — they're all blood, and when they die it all hurts the same. And there are other ways to cope with death besides drugs. You know I'm here for you like that. You've never talked to me about your feelings toward your mother's death. You've never even tried me. I'm your wife, Calvin. If you can't come to me and talk to me about your feelings, then what good am I? What good are we? I might as well pack up my bags and go back home."

"So, you leavin' me," he said, more of a statement rather than a question. And I found myself wondering if I should or not. *Should I?* I asked myself.

"Like I said, what good am I here?"

"I can beat this thing, Jay, if you just stick by my side … if you just hang in there."

"Calvin," I said, sighing. "That's about all we're doing, I'm afraid … is just hanging — by a thread. And you're beginning to sound like a broken record these days. Calvin, we have a son to raise. Correction, I'm going to work, paying the bills and busting my ass trying to raise our son … I don't have time to raise you, too. You're going to kill me if I let you keep this up. And I can't have that for C.J. I just can't. He deserves better. I deserve better."

"So, you leavin' me," he said again, slumping back against the couch and putting his hands behind his head.

"Calvin, I love you with all my heart. I want this marriage to work, but if I keep letting you run in and out like this, it's not going to. We're not going to make it. You've gotta go back into that rehab and get some help. Or we'll find another one, whatever. But we've got to break this pattern. It's not good."

"So you'll stay if I go back into the rehab?" he asked. I put my head between my knees and thought about his pleading. The entire time that we had been talking — or arguing, rather, I had been slowly convincing myself to break things off and run home. I was tired of fighting ... tired of the merry-go-round ... and really tired of the triangle I had found myself in. Ironically, I found myself wishing that I was competing against another woman — a real person instead of a thing. It would have made a lot more sense to me ... and would have made it easier to leave him. After a long pause, I answered him.

"Yes, Calvin. I'll stay — but only if you agree to go back for ninety days this time. I don't think thirty days was nearly long enough." I was expecting him to put up a big fight, but he surprised me.

"Okay," was all he said. Then he gave me a quick kiss on the forehead and got up, heading toward the kitchen. After a few minutes of rummaging around, he came back with a plate of spaghetti and breadsticks. I had been so busy ranting and raving, I hadn't even noticed any traces of cooking, but suddenly the aroma filled my nose and my mouth watered with a renewed hunger. He set the plate down on the coffee table in front of me and went back into the kitchen for a second plate, I thought. But when he came back, he was holding a bottle of wine and two goblets.

"What's all this?" I asked, a bit surprised.

"It's our anniversary," he said smiling.

"What? But Calvin, we've only been married for five months. We don't have an anniversary until next February."

"I'm not talkin' about that one. I'm talkin' about our other one. We've been together for two years and six months today." I looked at him and rolled my eyes.

"Calvin, normal people don't celebrate anniversaries like that. You at least have to go by the years ... or even the months, but on the same day each month, not sporadically as you see fit." He looked at me in an obvious stupor, which meant that he had no idea what I was talking about. I laughed and waved the subject off, not feeling like explaining any further. "Never mind, Calvin."

"Well, can't we celebrate me goin' back into rehab?" he asked. I laughed in spite of myself at the irony of that ... of all the things to open a bottle of wine for, all we had to celebrate was his drug habit.

"What's so funny? I'm tryin' to be serious and you keep makin' fun of me," he said, pouting like a little boy.

"Oh, honey, I'm not making fun of you. I just think some of your ideas are funny, that's all."

"Whatever," he said, finishing his glass of wine and pouring another. "I know you think I'm not serious, but I am. You'll see. Together, we can make it, if you just have a little more faith." I almost choked on a noodle with that comment, and as much as I wanted to reply, I didn't. Instead, I bit my tongue and washed down my food with a glass of wine to keep from saying anything damaging. Calvin was doing a hell of a job on his own without any help from me.

I swear, that boy never ceased to amaze me with some of the things he said. He had no idea how much faith I had. *If it weren't for my faith, we wouldn't have made it this far*, I thought to myself. *Hmph!* I poured myself another glass of wine and munched on a breadstick, marveling at all that had transpired in the last two and half years of my life.

* * * * *

In that little time frame, I had gone through enough hell to last anyone a lifetime, and more than enough to send someone to the loony bin. I believed that I had already lost my mind anyway, talking to myself all the time. In the last year, I had held memorable conversations and arguments with myself far more than I had with Calvin.

But when it all boiled down, I was still madly in love with the boy and would have given anything to stay with him, even my own life. And, in all honesty, that's just what I had done, given my life … my soul actually. No matter how crazy it sounded, I would come to realization that Calvin was right about the crack taking over his soul, because that's just what it had done, and in the process, Calvin had taken mine. I lived and breathed for him just as much as he lived and breathed for that pipe. We were a pitiful pair, the two of us. But right or wrong, we were man and wife, and that's what I hung on to, as thin as the thread was.

* * * * *

That night, Calvin coaxed me into making love, which wasn't too much of a task, considering how much wine I had consumed on a ravished stomach. The spaghetti was delicious, but was hardly enough nourishment after four days of withdrawal from food, so the wine went straight to my head. But that had been the plan all along, I imagined, and as always, it was sensational. It seemed with each argument our lovemaking became more intense, like the more we fought, the better we made love … strange, but true.

Chapter Eighteen

THE NEXT MORNING was a Friday, and I dreaded going into work for fear of coming home and finding Calvin gone again. But to my surprise, he was on time picking me up and we had a quiet weekend with C.J., watching old movies, cooking meals together and, of course, making love. It was a perfect weekend, and I would have considered it a turning point in our lives ... except for the fact that he would be leaving for the rehab again on Monday.

Naturally, he had lost his job, so that wasn't a factor in whether or not he should go through with the treatment. He had no excuses, and I wasn't backing down from our agreement. Of course, I would miss him terribly, but I took more countenance in the fact that it was for our own good rather than the fact that it would be three long months before I saw him again. By the time he returned home, our lease would be up. It was inevitable that we were not going to California anytime soon, not with one income supporting us. So I decided to go on with life as far as that dream was concerned and opted to settle for Tulsa as my new home. In November, we would renew our lease, this time for one whole year, and resume our marriage, once again.

Calvin was able to earn phone call privileges for up to thirty minutes each week, but most of the time frames for him to call were during my work hours. There was one block of time that started around noon, which worked with my lunch break, but by the time I made it back to the apartment and finished talking to him, I would push my time, trying to make it back to work within the hour. Susan had hinted about giving me a raise after only sixty days with the boutique. She had also implied a possible promotion to assistant manager, so I wasn't taking any chances on nixing my luck, and encouraged Calvin to correspond through letters. He didn't like it one bit, but couldn't argue with me considering that my job was the only thing keeping our household afloat.

I continued to walk to work, still working on my figure, although by then I had lost all of my baby fat, but just wanted to maintain things. I only used the car for longer trips such as going to the grocery store or taking C.J. across town to the park for an occasional push on the toddler swings. One day, while on my way home, a black car with tinted windows pulled up and started coasting alongside me.

The boutique was at the end of a strip mall of several other stores, so I thought nothing of it at first, thinking the driver was merely preparing to park. But when I finally came to the corner and turned left, the car also made a left, then stopped, and two large Black men emerged from the passenger doors. They were both wearing dark sunglasses, so I didn't recognize them at first. One of the men walked around and leaned on the car, and the other one slowly approached me. I thought for sure I was about to be mugged — or worse — and froze out of shock, not knowing what to do. The apartments were in eyeshot, but I had enough sense not to run toward them for fear of them finding out where I lived for a return visit, so I turned around and began walking the other direction, clutching tightly to my purse, but trying to remain calm. I didn't know if I should run or not. What did I know? I'd never been mugged before. It was broad daylight, so I really wasn't sure of their motives and did not want to do anything to aggravate them and wind up in the car myself. He started walking alongside me like it was the most natural thing in the world, and surprisingly, I mustered up enough spunk to stop walking and confront him. It was obvious I wasn't in any immediate danger, or I would have already been lying on the sidewalk without my purse ... or in the trunk of the car.

"Excuse me," I said, "can I help you?" He smiled and took his glasses off. It was Mr. Rawlins. "How ... how did you find us?" I asked uneasily, backing up against one of the buildings. He chuckled lightly and stepped back, presumably to let me know that he was not going to harm me.

"I'm not here to hurt you, ma'am. But, you know, your ole man's not that bright, so it was easy trackin' him down. I've been in town for a few days now. I was just waitin' for the right moment to approach *you*," he said. *Great*, I thought, *so he already knows where we live ... just great!*

"So, what do you want with me?" I asked. "Why haven't you talked to Calvin already?"

"Because I know he's not around right now, but I also know that the best way to reach him is through you."

"Well, I can't talk to him any more than you can right now," I said. "The only correspondence I have with him is through mail ..." *Damn!* I put my head down, scolding myself. *That was stupid, Jaycee ... really stupid! Now you're going to have to tell him where Calvin is ...*

"It's cool," he said, assuredly. "I already know where he's at — and good for him. You forget who I am, baby girl. I'm like God. There's no escapin' me." His man behind him started to laugh, and Rawlins joined him.

"Unh," I grunted, resenting his ill comparison. "Well,

you know I'd love to stand around and chat, but I have to get home," I said sarcastically, looking down at my watch. "As you also know, I have a son to take care of. So, again, I ask, what do you want from me?"

"Aww, yes," he recalled with a smile. "How is the little one? Hopefully, nothing like his daddy and more like you," he said, looking me up and down. I shuddered at his suggestive thoughts and tried to ignore his offensive ogling. Truth be told, he was actually a handsome older man, probably in his late thirties or early forties, with a distinguished goatee, slightly gray and naturally curly black hair. Lisa would have loved to have him for a client, and under different circumstances I might have entertained the thought myself. Suddenly, my face grew hot as I blushed internally, surprised at myself for even thinking such thoughts.

"Look, can't you just forget everything and let us get on with our lives?" I pleaded. "Calvin's no good to you now anyway. You know he's in the rehab, so he has no means of repaying your money back. You already took my engagement ring for collateral. What, you want this one, too?" I started to take my wedding ring off and hand it to him, but he fanned it away.

"Naw, baby girl." *God, I wish he'd stop calling me that,* I thought. "You can keep it this time. Besides, both of those rings together are hardly a dent in the amount that he took from me. I just want you to get a message to your little hubby. Tell him that he should really get in touch with me as soon as he gets out." He pulled a business card out of his suit pocket and handed it to me. "I have a little job for him, and if he does it for me, I'll forget about what he owes me and we can call it even." *Give me a break,* I thought. *A drug dealer with a business card? Well, if this doesn't beat all ...*

"What little job?"

"Nothing for you to worry about, sweet thing." I rolled my eyes at his reference to me. I didn't know why he was calling me all of those pet names, but it was starting to make my stomach turn. "If he does it for me, then your troubles will be over as far as any dealin's with me, and I'll never bother you again."

"And if he doesn't do what you want?"

"Well," he replied, smiling and gently taking my chin in his hand. "I would highly recommend that you encourage him to do it, pretty lady. Calvin knows the business and the rules of the game. Now, I've taken a likin' to you, so don't worry about yourself or your baby. I would never bring any harm your way, but rules are rules."

"Would you please take your hand off me," I said quietly, a tear rolling down my left cheek. "I understand now and I will tell him what you said."

"You do that, sweetheart," he said, smiling and stepping back. He bowed and stuck his arm out as if he were an usher, permitting me to walk by. I wiped the tear away abruptly and charged past him with my head up, looking straight ahead.

"Bye, baby girl!" he called, getting back into the car. I kept walking without even looking back or answering him.

When I made it to the apartments, I raced up the steps, got C.J. and went straight to Lisa's.

"Lisa!" I yelled, frantically pounding on the door. "Lisa, let me in! Li —"

"Okay, okay," she said, throwing the door open and yanking me in. Instinctively peeked her head around the corner, as if she were expecting to find a predator in my shadows, she locked the door behind her a few minutes later.

"What is it? Was someone following you?"

"Kind of," I said. "Sorry, I didn't mean to startle you."

"Really? Well, that was a very poor example of how

not to startle someone," she said. "What's up? Who was followin' you?" She walked over to the couch where I was sitting, holding onto C.J. for dear life, and sat down beside me.

"Rawlins," I said.

"Rawlins? Who's that?"

"The drug dealer from Kansas, remember? Calvin used to work for him."

Lisa nodded her head, recalling the story I told her.

"I thought we had gotten rid of him, but apparently not. He stopped me on my home from work and told me to get a message to Calvin and that he has to do what he says or there will be trouble because *'rules are rules.'* "

"You mean Calvin fucked him over and now he wants his, but since Calvin doesn't have any, he has do to do a job for him, and if he doesn't go along with it, he's gonna kill him." I looked at her in awe, wondering how she knew and had figured everything out so fast.

"How did you know?"

"It kinda goes with the territory, love. Calvin knows the business."

"That's exactly what Rawlins said."

"It's true, Jay. Look, I'm sorry he stepped to you like that. He didn't hurt you, did he?" she asked, looking me over.

"No, I'm fine. He was actually very nice to me and gentle in a sick kind of way," I said, recalling him touching my chin and using all of those pet names. "He kept calling me baby girl and sweetheart and all of these pet names like I was his girlfriend or something. It was very disgusting."

"Yeah, they're real Casanovas, those types."

"How can they be so sweet like that, considering what they do?" I asked. "I mean, they kill people … literally … firsthand and secondhand through their drugs. Then they can turn around and be all kind and gentle to a woman, just like that? I mean, he acted like he would have taken me to bed if I had let him. I'm actually surprised that wasn't part of the deal."

"Shut up before you jinx yourself," Lisa said.

"No, he wouldn't dare."

"He would, Jaycee. Don't ever question that or put anything past those people. That's the kind of lives they lead. And if Calvin doesn't straighten up and get clean, he'll be pimpin' you and hisself out ..."

"Stop!" I yelled. "That will never happen, you hear me? Not as long as I'm alive. I'll die first."

"Jaycee, baby, this thing is bigger than Calvin made it out to be. When he first called and told me what was goin' down and that y'all needed a place to stay, he didn't go into much detail and I didn't ask. I wish I would have. But he was family and y'all had a baby, so that was enough for me, right there. I love Calvin with all my heart, but I think you should cut your losses now while you got a chance. Take your baby and go back home to your parents. Calvin has no business bringin' you or me into this shit. I got kids; you have a child. We have to protect ourselves and them."

"What are you saying? You think I should leave Calvin ... just leave him to die?"

"He won't die. Business is business, and Calvin will know what to do when he gets out of rehab. I'm not sayin' leave him for good, but give him somethin' to think about, you know what I mean? He ain't gonna really change as long as he knows you're gonna always be there, right by his side. He needs to know that you *ain't* gonna always be around if he keeps all this up. He needs to hit rock bottom — on his own ... and only then he'll wake up and shape up." I couldn't say anything in response. I just kept shaking my head back and forth, crying quietly.

"How can I leave him now?" I asked after a while. "... when he's at his worst? Isn't that kind of low? I couldn't do that to him. I wouldn't want him to do it to me. And you're the one that's always saying *stand by your man*," I mocked. "What happened to all that talk, hunh?"

"Jaycee," she said holding my head up to look at her. "Look at me. I'm only telling you this for your own good. I told you all that because I thought Calvin was clean. He so much as swore it to me. Under normal circumstances, yes, you do stand by your man — when he's about somethin', takin' care of home and doin' you right. Even when you catch your man in a little lie, if you know he means well, then that makes all the difference. But Calvin doesn't mean well right now. He's sick and you're not a doctor. You can't help him. The actual doctors at that rehab can't help him. Like I've told you before, Calvin is his own doctor. He has to be a man now and save hisself. You have to stop being hero and start being a mother to that baby — and don't take that the wrong way," she said, stopping me before I got started with a rebuttal. She must have seen the look on my face.

"I didn't mean it like that," she said. "I just meant that you need to keep focus on what's important, and now that you're a mother, that takes priority over any man, I don't care who or what he is."

"He's my husband."

"And what is C.J.?"

"I know he's my son, but if it weren't for Calvin, he wouldn't be here."

"Girl, please. He would've been here, his name would've just been somethin' else besides Calvin, Jr." I looked at her a little bewildered, and she sighed and rolled her eyes at me in disgust. "If it weren't for my stupid-ass cousin, you might've met a halfway decent man and had a normal life right now without all the drama.

C.J. would've just been by somebody else, that's all. Calvin is not the only man in the world who knows how to make a baby, Jaycee."

"I know that!" I snapped.

"Look, just go home and rest and give it some thought. We can talk about it some more tomorrow when we both get off work."

"Can we stay here tonight?" I asked. "It kind of gives me the creeps knowing that Rawlins might be watching me. He admitted that he'd been in town for a few days already, and he knows where I work. I'm pretty sure he knows which apartment I live in, too."

"I'm sure he does, but like you said, he didn't hurt you. If he wanted to, he could have and I'm sure he would have already approached you at your place by now if that's what he wanted. But you know you're always welcome here, love."

Chapter Nineteen

So C.J. AND I stayed there at Lisa's that night, and I went to work the following morning as if nothing ever happened. All day, I thought about what she had said about leaving Calvin. I couldn't believe that she had suggested such a thing. Of all people, I never expected Calvin's own relative to turn on him and give me a piece of advice like that. I had thought that blood was always thicker than water, but Lisa Jones had instilled in me a new concept regarding traditional adages like that. It never occurred to me then, but that night she had taught me a new principle ... a thing called *sisterhood*.

We weren't sisters, we weren't even related except by marriage. But we were both two Black women ... two black mothers. We were both young and struggling to survive with our children. We had both been in love, then in pain ... her a few more times than me perhaps, and under different circumstances, but all in all, we were still the same. And from one sister to another, no matter how much I hated to hear her when she was trying to give me advice on Calvin, she was only trying to feed me a little of her wisdom from past experiences in hope that I might learn from her and better my situation.

Through Lisa, I would come to realization that one truly can't *live on love* and that a man isn't everything.

* * * * *

After work, I went home and sat down at the kitchen table to write a letter to Calvin. When I finished, I had written almost ten pages, front and back. I folded it up and sealed it in an envelope, along with Rawlins' business card. When I finished, I walked over to the phone and called the operator to place a long-distance call. It seemed like the phone rang for hours, and just when I was about to hang up, someone answered.

"Hello?"

"Mom?"

"Jaycee?" she whispered. "Baby, is that you?"

"Yeah, Mom," I smiled with tears in my eyes. "Mom, I'm tired." There was a long pause and then she answered me.

"I'll leave the porch light on for you and go make the bed up in the spare room ..." I burst into tears and cried uncontrollably. She never said a word after that the whole time I was having my fit. I was in complete misery ... at *my* rock bottom, I imagined. My marriage had failed, and I had completely alienated myself from my parents for almost two years without so much as a postcard. There had been no contact at all, and for me to just have the gall to call her and ask to come home, and for her to comply, no questions asked, had just overwhelmed me into hysterics. I was heavy with shame.

"What about Dad?" I asked after I had calmed myself down.

"He'll be fine. Just give him some time, but he's still your father no matter what. He'll always love you."

* * * * *

I went into the work the next morning early so I could have time to talk to Susan and tell her why it would be my last day. I had thought about telling her the whole dreaded story, but changed my mind and made up a lie about my father suddenly taking ill and needing to go back home. Naturally, she was crushed and suggested that I take a leave of absence rather than quit, hoping that I would plan on returning at some point. She even offered to continue my wages while I was away, but I graciously declined, feeling the shame all over again as I had with my mother the night before. My guilt pierced me like I would imagine a knife wound felt ... sharp, unbearable pains ... much like contractions to a woman about to give birth.

I went home and packed up our clothes, leaving only the furniture from the living room and a few pictures on the wall. Calvin had taken the majority of his clothes with him, and what was left I bagged up and gave to Lisa. There was one month left in the lease, of which I had already paid up, so Lisa had made arrangements to have the rest of the furniture and knick-knacks moved to her place at the end of the month.

I was still having a hard time dealing with the raw fact that I was abandoning my husband, but Lisa was right ... I had to get out now before it was too late. It was too dangerous to stay and keep fighting Calvin's battles for him, but even more dangerous to believe what Rawlins had said about not hurting me.

"Eventually, that will be null and void," Lisa had said. "If Calvin's not completely clean this time when he gets out and messes up with Rawlins again, it will be no holds barred and he'll hurt Calvin without even laying a finger on him ... he'll get to him through you ... or worse, the baby."

* * * * *

That was the deciding factor for my decision to leave, after hearing her say that. It was like coming out of a coma after being asleep for two years. I had been hearing her voice all along, but I had not comprehended what she was saying. But suddenly, everything was crystal clear. And the truth had hit me like a mack truck. All along I had been following Lisa's advice to stand by Calvin and support him, which I had always done. But she had also been trying to teach me something that I had not understood when my mother had tried to talk to me that day in the kitchen.

"... Love compromises – not jeopardizes. If a situation arises, love stands ground and deals with the problem ... not runs or drags other people into it who have no business ..." That's what Mom had said, and she had been right.

They had both been right, trying to teach me the same principle, to have a sense of self ... self-respect, self-worth, self-love. Hearing it from my mother was too much like a lecture. And everyone knows that the more your parents try to keep you from something, the closer they draw you to it. But hearing it from Lisa who was my peer made it easier to grasp, I guess ...

> "...and we know that all things work together for good to them that love God, to them who are the called according to his purpose."
> — Romans 8:28
> King James Version

Epilogue

ON MY WAY back home to Kansas, I wondered if Calvin would ever bring himself to understand and forgive me for leaving him. I wondered if I would ever forgive him for all that he had put me through. I hoped that, in time, we both would learn to forgive each other and get past everything, that we would both gain a sense of *self* and renew ourselves. In the letter, I advised him to ask permission to stay longer than the three months. After learning that his drug addiction had been an ongoing illness and not as recent as I had thought, I anticipated that he needed extensive treatment, possibly even for a whole year.

Lisa had told me not to worry about him, and that she would sit down and talk to him on my behalf and admit to him that it had been her idea for me to go. She said that, in time, he would understand and at least whatever bitterness or anger he had would be directed towards her, so that by the time he was ready to start over with me, it would be on a clean slate all the way around.

I never mentioned to her that I had reservations about us starting over as soon as he came out. I hoped that she was right about the bitterness and anger part being over before I had to deal with him, but I wasn't so sure that we could resume as we were just like that. That would definitely take some time even after Calvin was back from rehab.

* * * * *

I was received with much love and welcome arms from my parents.

My father didn't say much, but I could see in his eyes that he was glad to have me back home. And his hug told me everything I needed to know despite his lack of words. But Mom made up for his silence as she fussed over my weight loss, claiming I looked malnourished and must not have been eating right. In the same breath, she couldn't get over how much C.J. had grown and delighted herself in biting his chubby cheeks and pinching the fat on his legs.

Fortunately, I had left my old job at the insurance firm on good terms, and I was able to go back to work immediately. They resumed my pay and benefits as if I'd never left. Mom took care of C.J. while I worked, and Dad took me car shopping after my first paycheck, and I traded in the Honda for a newer model with four doors. My new car proved to be more accessible than the other one for transporting C.J. back and forth in the carseat, and I loved it. I also liked having a fresh start in the new car, along with my new life away from Calvin. I no longer had to worry about it being a target for cops or old drug associates of Calvin's.

Calvin continued to write me, professing his undying love for me and swearing that he would be a new man once he got out of the rehab. I took everything he said with a grain of salt, answering each letter sparingly, while continuing my own journey to a better life without thugs and drugs. It was nice living a simple life, free of worry and without all of the drama I had witnessed in the past two years. I even contemplated divorce, but instead decided to file for a legal separation until Calvin was out of rehab. We both had a lot of growing up to do, Calvin more than me, of course, but the next time I wanted things to be completely different, and the only way I could see to that was with time ... a lot of time.

Sometimes things don't always work out the way you want them to or even expect them to. But God has a way of showing up just at the right time; whether you choose to see or hear him is up to you.